# BOB THE CASTAWAY

Or, The Wreck of the Eagle

FRANK V. WEBSTER

1st WORLD
LIBRARY
Literary Society

# Bob the Castaway

## Frank V. Webster

© 1st World Library, 2006
PO Box 2211
Fairfield, IA 52556
www.1stworldlibrary.com
First Edition

LCCN: 2006937747

Softcover ISBN: 978-1-4218-3328-6
Hardcover ISBN: 978-1-4218-3228-9
eBook ISBN: 978-1-4218-3428-3

Purchase *"Bob the Castaway"*
as a traditional bound book at:
www.1stWorldLibrary.com/purchase.asp?ISBN=978-1-4218-3328-6

1st World Library is a literary, educational organization
dedicated to:

- Creating a free internet library of downloadable ebooks

- Hosting writing competitions and offering book
  publishing scholarships.

**Interested in more 1st World Library books?**
contact: literacy@1stworldlibrary.com
**Check us out at: www.1stworldlibrary.com**

# 1ˢᵗ World Library Literary Society

## Giving Back to the World

"If you want to work on the core problem, it's early school literacy."

**- James Barksdale, former CEO of Netscape**

"No skill is more crucial to the future of a child, or to a democratic and prosperous society, than literacy."

**- Los Angeles Times**

Literacy... means far more than learning how to read and write... The aim is to transmit... knowledge and promote social participation."

**- UNESCO**

"Literacy is not a luxury, it is a right and a responsibility. If our world is to meet the challenges of the twenty-first century we must harness the energy and creativity of all our citizens."

**- President Bill Clinton**

"Parents should be encouraged to read to their children, and teachers should be equipped with all available techniques for teaching literacy, so the varying needs and capacities of individual kids can be taken into account."

**- Hugh Mackay**

# CONTENTS

# CHAPTER I

## BOB MAKES TROUBLE

"Bob! Bob!" called a woman in loud tones, as she came to the kitchen door, her arms, with the sleeves rolled up to her elbows, covered with flour. "Bob, I want you to go to the store for me. I need some more lard for this pie-crust."

There was no answer, and the woman looked across the big yard at one side of the cottage.

"Where can that boy be?" Mrs. Henderson murmured. "I saw him here a little while ago. He's never around when I want him. I shouldn't be surprised but what he was planning some joke. Oh, dear! I wish he was more steady, and wasn't always up to some mischief. Still, he's a good boy at heart, and perhaps he'll grow better when he gets older."

She rubbed her left cheek with the back of her hand, leaving a big patch of flour under one eye. Then she called once more.

"Bob! Bob Henderson! Where are you? I want you to go to the store."

"Here I am, mother. Were you calling me?" asked a boy, emerging from behind a big apple tree.

He was not a bad-looking lad, even if his nose did turn up a bit, though his hair was tinged with red, and his face covered with freckles. His blue eyes, however, seemed to sparkle with mischief.

"Did I call you?" repeated Mrs. Henderson. "I'm hoarse after the way I had to shout—and you within hearing distance all the while! Why didn't you answer me?"

"I guess I was so busy thinking, mom, that I didn't hear you."

"Thinking? More likely thinking of some trick! What's that you've got?"

"Nothing," and Bob tried to stuff pieces of paper into a basket that was already filled to overflowing.

"Yes, 'tis too something. You're making some more of those paper snappers that the teacher kept you in after school for the other night. Bob, can't you settle down and not be always up to some trick?"

"I wasn't making these for myself, mom, honest I wasn't," expostulated Bob, with an innocent look that did not seem in accord with the mischief in his blue eyes. "I was making 'em for Jimmy Smith."

"Yes, and Jimmy Smith would pop 'em off in school, and when he got caught he'd say you gave 'em to him, and you'd both be kept in. Oh, Bob, I don't know what will happen to you next!"

"Why, I wasn't doing anything, honest I wasn't, mom. Oh, how funny you look with that patch of flour on your cheek! Just like a clown in a circus, only he has white stuff all over his face."

"Well, I must say, Bob Henderson, you're not very complimentary to your mother, telling her she looks like a circus clown."

"I didn't say you did, mom. You only look like half a clown."

"That's just as bad."

Bob took advantage of this little diversion to hide the paper snappers behind the tree while his mother was wiping the flour off her face. The snappers were oblong pieces of stout wrapping paper, folded in such a way that when swung through the air they went off like a bag blown up and crushed between the hands. Bob was an expert in their manufacture.

"Come," went on Mrs. Henderson, when she was satisfied that her face was no longer adorned with flour, "I want you to go to the store for some lard. Tell Mr. Hodge you want the best. Here's the money."

"All right, mom, I'll go right away. Do you want anything else?"

Now Bob usually made more of a protest than this when asked to go to the store, which was at the other end of the village of Moreville, where he lived. He generally wanted to stay at his play, or was on the point of going off with some boy of his acquaintance.

But this time he prepared to go without making any complaint, and had his mother not been so preoccupied thinking of her housework, she might have suspected that the lad had some mischief afoot—some scheme that he wanted to carry out, and which going to the store would further.

"No, I guess the lard is all I need now," she said. "Now do hurry, Bob. Don't stop on the way, for I want to get these pies baked before supper."

"I'll hurry, mom."

There was a curious smile on Bob's face, and as he got his hat from the ground before setting off on the errand he looked in his pocket to see if he had a certain long, stout piece of cord.

"I guess that will do the trick," murmured the boy to himself. "Oh, yes, I'll hurry back all right! Guess I'll have to if I don't want Bill Hodge to catch me."

There was a cunning look on Bob's face, and the twinkle in his eyes increased as he set off down the village street.

"I hope he doesn't get into mischief," murmured Mrs. Henderson, as she went back to her work in the kitchen. "If he wasn't such an honest boy, I would be more worried than I am about him. But I guess he will outgrow it," she added hopefully.

Bob Henderson, who is to be the hero of our Story, was the only son of Mr. and Mrs. Enos Henderson. They lived in Moreville, a thriving New England town, and Bob's father was employed in a large woolen mill in the place.

Bob attended the local school, and he was a sort of leader among a certain class of boys. They were all manly chaps, but perhaps were inclined more to mischief than they should be. And none of them was any more inclined that way than Bob. He was rather wild, and some of the things he did were unkind and harmful to those on whom he played jokes.

Bob was always the first to acknowledge he had been in the wrong, and when it was pointed out to him that he had not done what was right he always apologized. Only this was always after the mischief had been done, and he was just as ready half an hour later to indulge in another prank.

Nearly every one In Moreville knew Bob, some to their sorrow. But in spite of his tricks he was well liked, even though some nervous women predicted that he would land in jail before he got to be much older.

It was a pleasant afternoon In June, and Bob had not been

home from school long when his mother sent him after the lard. As it happened, this just suited the youth's purpose, for he contemplated putting into operation a trick he had long planned against William Hodge, the proprietor of the village grocery store.

So Bob trudged along, whistling a merry tune and jingling in his pocket the money his mother had given him.

"He'll be as mad as hops," he murmured, "but it can't do much harm. He'll turn it off before much runs out."

This may seem rather a puzzle to my young readers, but if you have patience you will soon understand what Bob meant, though I hope none of you will follow his example.

As Bob walked along he met another lad about his own age.

"Hello, Bob," greeted Ted Neefus. "Where you goin'?"

"Store."

"What store?"

"Bill Hodge's."

"What fer?"

"Lard."

"Want me t' go 'long?"

"If you want to," and there was a half smile on Bob's face. Ted knew the meaning of that smile. He had more than once been associated with Bob in his tricks.

"Kin I watch ye?" he asked eagerly.

"What for?" asked Bob with an air of assumed indignation.

"What do you think I'm going to do?"

"Oh, that's all right," returned Ted. "I won't say anythin'. Let me watch, will yer?"

"I don't s'pose I can stop you," replied Bob, with an appearance of lofty virtue. "The street's public property. I haven't any right to say you shan't stand in front of Bill's store until I come out. You can if you want to."

"Maybe I won't then!" exclaimed Ted.

"Better not walk along with me," advised Bob. "Folks might think we were up to something."

"That's so. Like when we burned some feathers under the church when they were having prayer meeting."

"Don't speak so loud," cautioned Bob. "You'll give things away."

Thus admonished, Ted took a position well to his chum's rear. Meanwhile Bob continued on and was soon at the grocery store.

"Good-afternoon, Mr. Hodge," he said politely.

"Arternoon," replied Mr. Hodge, for he was not fond of boys, least of all Bob Henderson. "What d' you want?"

He had an air as if he was saying:

"Now none of your tricks, you young rapscallion! If you play any jokes on me you'll smart for it!"

"Mother wants a pound of lard—the best lard, Mr. Hodge," said Bob.

"I don't keep any but the best."

"Then I want a pound. It's a fine day, isn't it?"

"I don't see nothin' the matter with it. 'Tain't rainin' anyhow. Now don't you upset anything while I go fer the lard. I have t' keep it down cellar, it's so hot up here."

Bob knew this. In fact, he counted on it for what he was about to do. No sooner had the storekeeper started down the cellar stairs than Bob pulled from his pocket a long, stout piece of cord. He quickly fastened one end of it to the spigot of a molasses barrel, which stood about half way back in the store. Then he ran the cord forward and across the doorway, about six inches from the floor, and fastened the other end to a barrel of flour as a sort of anchor.

By this time Mr. Hodge was coming upstairs with the lard in a thin wooden dish, a piece of paper being over the top. Bob stood near the counter piling the scale weights up in a regular pyramid.

"Here, let them alone," growled the storekeeper. "Fust thing you know they'll fall an' mebby crack."

"I wouldn't have that happen," said Bob earnestly, but with a lurking smile on his lips. "How much is the lard, Mr. Hodge?"

"Fourteen cents. It's gone up."

"Something else will be going down soon," murmured Bob.

He paid over the money, took the lard and started out. As soon as he reached the front stoop of the store he gave a hasty look around. He saw Ted dodging behind a tree across the street. Suddenly Bob opened his mouth and let out a yell like that which an Indian might have given when on the warpath. It was a shriek as if some one had been hurt. Then he jumped off the porch and hid underneath it, one end being open.

An instant later Mr. Hodge, thinking some accident had

happened, rushed to the front door of his store. But just as he reached it he went down in a heap, tripped by the string Bob had stretched across the opening.

The storekeeper was more surprised than hurt, for he was quite stout and his fat protected him. As he got up, muttering vengeance on whatever had upset him, he went to the door to look out. There was not a person in sight.

"It must have been that pesky Bob Henderson!" he exclaimed. "He's always yellin' an' shoutin'."

He turned back into the store, rubbing his shins. As he did so he uttered an exclamation of dismay. And well he might, for the spigot of the molasses barrel was wide open, and the sticky brown fluid was running all over the floor.

Frank V. Webster

# CHAPTER II

## ANOTHER PRANK

"Drat that boy!" cried Mr. Hodge. "I'll make him suffer fer this. I'll have him arrested fer malicious mischief, an' I'll sue his father. I'll see if I can't put a stop to sech nonsense."

He did not waste time in words, however, but hastened to shut the spigot of the molasses barrel to stop the wasteful flow. However, two gallons or more had run all over, the floor, making a sticky pool.

Meanwhile Bob had crawled out from under the stoop and had crossed the street to Join Ted.

"Did you see anything?" he asked.

"Did I?" asked Ted. "Well, I should say I did. It was great. How'd ye think of it?"

"Did I do anything?" asked Bob innocently. "I thought Bill Hodge stubbed his toe and fell. Probably he slipped in some molasses."

"Did you pull the spigot open?"

"Me? No, I didn't, but maybe the string did. I guess I've got to hurry home with this lard. Mom wants to make some pies."

Bob got home much sooner than his mother expected he would. He gave her the lard, and then went out under the apple tree where he had left the paper snappers.

"He's back quick," mused Mrs. Henderson. "I don't see how he had time to do any mischief. Perhaps he didn't play any tricks on any one this time," for Bob seldom went through the village but what he did so. However, Mrs. Henderson was mistaken, as we know.

During this time Mr. Hodge was busy wiping as much of the molasses off the floor as he could with old cloths and pieces of newspaper. While he was doing this a customer came in and inquired:

"What's the matter? Molasses barrel spring a leak, Bill?"

"Leak? No, it was that pesky Bob Henderson. Wait till I git hold of him! I'll make him smart. An' I'm goin' to sue his father."

"What did he do? Why, Bill, you walk lame. What's the matter, got rheumatiz?"

"It's all on account of Bob."

"What did he do?"

"Came here for some lard. When I was down cellar gittin' it he tied a string to the molasses barrel spigot and stretched it across the doorway."

"What, the spigot?"

"No, the string. Ye know what I mean. Then he went out on the stoop an' yelled like sin. I thought somebody was killed an' I run out. I tripped over the string an' it pulled the spigot open. I barked my shins, an' when I looked in the store, after seein' nobody was hurt, the molasses was runnin' all over. Oh, wait till I git hold of that pesky boy!"

"I s'pose if you hadn't been so curious to see who was killed it wouldn't have happened," observed Adiran Meelik.

"Curious! Ain't I got a right to run an' see who's killed in front of my store?"

"I s'pose so. But there wasn't anybody killed; only you came near being."

"That's so. I'll bring an action against Bob Henderson's father for damages for personal injuries, that's what I'll do. Then there's the wasted molasses."

"That boy plays too many tricks," observed Mr. Meelik as he took the brown sugar he had come in to purchase and walked out. "Altogether too many tricks. Still," he added with a smile, "I would like to have seen Bill stumble and watched his face when he seen that molasses runnin' to waste."

The storekeeper lost no time in putting his plan into action. But as he was a cautious man, and did not want to waste money hiring a lawyer to bring suit if he could collect damages without doing so, he decided to call on Mr. Henderson himself.

A short time after Mr. Hodge had succeeded in cleaning up as much of the molasses as possible his wife came in to relieve him of tending the store, as was her custom. She had had an early supper, and was to remain in the place until Mr. Hodge had also satisfied his appetite. By this arrangement there was no need of hiring a clerk. They lived in some rooms over the store.

"Your supper's ready, William," she said.

"I guess supper'll have to wait to-night."

"Why?"

"'Cause I'm goin' to see if I can't collect damages from Enos Henderson fer what his son done."

"What's that?"

Mr. Hodge explained, and his wife agreed with him that it would be wise first to try what a personal demand would do.

It was about six o'clock when Mr. Hodge reached the Henderson home. Mr. Henderson stopped work at five, and he was at supper when the storekeeper entered. Bob knew the object of the visit, and, making an excuse that he wanted to see one of his boy chums, was about to leave the table.

"My business is with him, too," said Mr. Hodge in rather surly tones.

"With Bob?" asked Mr. Henderson, and his heart sank. He realized that his son must have been up to some prank in which the storekeeper was involved, for Mr. Hodge was not a person to pay friendly calls.

"Yes. I've come t' see if ye'll settle my claim fer damages without a lawsuit."

"A lawsuit?" inquired Mr. Henderson, now becoming quite alarmed, while Bob's mother grew pale. Bob himself, not a little frightened as the result of his joke, sank down in a chair,

"I want damages fer personal injuries, as well as fer five gallons of molasses that run to waste."

"It couldn't have been more than three gallons," interrupted Bob. "Molasses runs awful slow, and the spigot wasn't open more than three minutes."

"It runs fast in hot weather," observed the storekeeper.

"What is it all about?" asked Mr. Henderson.

Then Mr. Hodge explained, dwelling on the pain he had suffered as a result of the fall from the string that tripped him and on the loss of the molasses.

"I want ten dollars damage," he concluded. "A dollar fer the molasses an' the rest fer personal injuries."

"I am afraid I cannot afford to pay so much," said Mr. Henderson, who, while he made good wages, was trying to save up enough to pay for his home.

"Then I'll sue ye."

"I would not like you to do that, but I cannot afford to pay ten dollars—at least not now. I have some interest to meet this week."

"Well, maybe I might take a little less," said Mr. Hodge, as he saw a prospect of Bob's father coming to a settlement. "I'll make it eight dollars, an' ye can pay me in installments."

"I suppose that will be fair," admitted Mr. Henderson. He spoke very quietly, but he was much exercised over what had happened.

"Can ye pay me anythin' now?" asked Mr. Hodge eagerly, rubbing his shins, which, to tell the truth, were only slightly bruised and did not hurt him in the least now.

"I could give you two dollars. But first I want to ask Bob if he is responsible for this."

To his sorrow Mr. Henderson did not have much doubt of it.

"Oh, I guess he won't deny it," said the storekeeper.

"Did you do this, Bob?" inquired his father.

"I—I guess so, but I didn't mean anything."

Bob was not so happy over his prank as he had been at first.

Mr. Henderson said nothing. He took two dollars from his wallet—a wallet that did not have any too much money in it—and handed the bills to the storekeeper, who eagerly pocketed them.

"When kin ye give me some more?" he asked.

"Next week. I am sorry, Mr. Hodge, that my son did this."

"So am I. But I s'pose boys will be boys."

Mr. Hodge seemed in better mood. The truth was, he had not expected to receive any money, and as he was a sort of miser, it made him feel better to think he was going to get damages without having to pay a lawyer. In reality, not more than fifty cents' worth of molasses had run to waste.

When the storekeeper had left Mr. Henderson further questioned Bob, getting all the particulars of the trick.

"I'm sorry, dad," said Bob when he had finished his recital.

"That is what you say every time, my son. You said it after you frightened Mrs. Anderson's cow and they had to have the veterinarian for the animal, but that did not pay his bill. I had to settle for it,"

"I know, dad. I'll not do it again."

"And that's another thing you always say, Bob. Now this is getting serious. You must mend your ways. This will be quite a heavy expense to me. I was going to spend that two dollars for a new pair of shoes. Now I will have to wait."

"I'm sorry, dad."

"But that doesn't give me my shoes,"

Mr. Henderson spoke gravely, and Bob felt quite badly over what he had done, for he loved his father and mother very much, and would not intentionally pain them. The trouble was he was, like many other boys, thoughtless. He did not count the consequences when indulging in pranks.

A little later, after giving his son quite a severe lecture, and obtaining his promise to be better in the future, Mr. Henderson prepared to go to bed. Bob also retired to his room, for he felt in no mood to go out with the village boys that night.

"I'm sure I don't know what to do with Bob," said Mrs. Henderson to her husband when she was locking up the house. "I'm afraid he'll get into serious trouble."

"I hope not. I think I must punish him severely the next time he plays any tricks."

"He is too big to whip."

"I know it. I must think of some other method."

Bob fell asleep, resolving to mend his ways, or at least to play in the future only harmless tricks to which no one would object. But in the morning his good resolutions had lost some of their power, like many others made during the night.

That day in school Bob snapped several of the paper crackers, and in consequence was kept in. However, his mother was visiting a neighbor, and when he came home late that afternoon she did not see him.

That evening Ted Neefus called for Bob. They were chums of long standing.

"Let's take a walk," suggested Ted.

"Aw, that's no fun."

"What'll we do then?"

Bob thought a few seconds.

"I'll tell you," he said. "We'll put a tic-tac on Mrs. Mooney's window. She lives all alone, and she'll think it's a ghost rapping."

"Good! Come on. Have you got some string?"

"Sure."

So you see how poorly Bob remembered his promise of the night before, and with what thoughtlessness he again started to indulge in a prank—a prank which might throw a nervous woman into hysterics. Yet in this Bob was just like thousands of other boys—he "didn't mean anything." The trouble was he did not think.

So the two boys, their heads full of the project of making a tic-tac, stole quietly through the village streets toward the cottage of the Widow Mooney.

## CHAPTER III

## A STRANGE PROPOSITION

Perhaps some of my readers may not know what the contrivance known as a "tic-tac" is like. Those of you who have made them, of course, do not need to be told. If you ever put them on any person's window, I hope you selected a house where there were only boys and girls or young people to be startled by the tic-tac. It is no joke, though at first it may seem like one, to scare an old person with the affair. So if any boy or girl makes a tic-tac after the description given here, I trust he or she will be careful on whom the prank is played.

To make a tic-tac a long string, a pin and a small nail are all that is required. A short piece of string is broken from the larger piece, and to one end of this latter the pin is fastened by being thrust through a knot.

To the other end or the short cord is attached the nail. Then the long string is tied to the short string a little distance above the nail.

With this contrivance all made ready Bob and Ted sneaked up under the front window of the widow's house. It was the work of but a moment for Bob to stick the point of the pin in the wooden part of the window-frame so that the nail dangled against the glass. Then, holding the free end of the long string, he and Ted withdrew to the shadow of some lilac bushes.

"All ready?" asked Ted.

"Sure. Here she goes!"

Bob then gently jerked the string. This swung the nail to and fro, and it tapped on the window-pane as if some one was throwing pebbles against the glass. This was kept up for several seconds.

The widow, who was reading in the dining-room, heard the tapping at the glass. It startled her at first, and then, thinking some one might be at the door, she conquered her nervousness and opened the portal. Of course she saw no one, and the string was not observed. Neither were the boys, hidden in the bushes.

"We fooled her," chuckled Ted, for they could see all that happened.

"Sure we did," added Bob. "Wait till she goes in and we'll do it some more."

Somewhat puzzled, the Widow Mooney closed the door. No sooner was she back in the dining-room than the tapping at the pane was resumed. This time it was louder. The widow, who was quite timid and nervous, felt frightened. She had years before believed in spirits, and she had not altogether gotten over this.

Once more she went to the door, the boys observing her from their hiding-place. They were so delighted with their prank, which they thought a fine "joke," that they laughed heartily, having to hold their hands over their mouths so as not to betray themselves.

"She don't know what it is," whispered Ted.

"Maybe she thinks it's night-hawks pecking at the window," suggested Bob.

"Go ahead. Tap some more. She's going in."

Much puzzled by the queer noises, for no one had ever before put a tic-tac on her window, Mrs. Mooney went back to her dining-room. But she could not read.

"I must find out what that is," she said to herself. "If it's burglars, I'm going to call for help. Suppose it should be thieves trying to cut one of the window-panes? I've read of such doings."

Now, the widow was less afraid of something bodily, like burglars, than she was of "spirits," so she resolved the next time she heard the queer tapping to run out and call for help.

In a little while Bob pulled the string again, and the dangling nail went tap! tap! tap! against the pane.

"Here she comes!" exclaimed Ted in a whisper as the door opened.

And this time, instead of contenting herself by merely looking about, Mrs. Mooney came out on the porch. Then she started down the front walk toward the lilac bushes, though she did not know the boys were there.

"She's comin' after us," whispered Ted. "Come on, Bob."

Bob was aware of the danger of getting caught. He prepared to run.

Now there is this advantage to a tic-tac. Once you want to escape you can take it with you by the simple process of pulling on the long string, when the pin is jerked from the window-frame, and you can drag the nail and all with you, thus leaving no evidence behind. This was what Bob did.

Quickly winding up die string as he pulled the pin and nail toward him, he and Ted started to run, crouching down low so as not to be seen. But Ted, unfortunately for the success of their plan, stumbled and fell, making so much noise that Mrs. Mooney heard t.

"Thieves! Burglars! Police!" she screamed.

"Come on!" cried Bob desperately. "We'll be caught!"

Mrs. Mooney ran back into the house, slammed the front door, shut and locked it. She believed she had surprised thieves at work, for she saw two dim forms running toward the street.

"Leg it!" whispered Bob.

"I am," replied Ted.

They reached the gate together, but that was as far as they got, for just as they arrived at it they collided with a large man who was running toward the house. He was so large that the combined impact of Bob and Ted against him never staggered him, but it almost threw them off their feet. They were running, head down, and had not seen him.

"Hold hard there, my hearties!" exclaimed the man in a gruff but not unpleasant voice. "What are you trying to cross my bows for in this fashion? That's no way to run, not showing a masthead light or even blowing a whistle. Avast and belay! You might have sunk me if I didn't happen to be a heavier craft than you."

As the man spoke he instinctively grasped the two boys, preventing them from continuing their flight.

"What's the trouble?" he went on. "I heard a female crying— sounding a distress signal like. Where are the burglars? Are you going for the police?"

"No, sir. It was us, playing tic-tac," explained Bob, thinking it best to make a clean breast of the affair.

"Tic-tac, eh? I haven't heard that since I was a boy. On whose window?"

"The Widow Mooney's, sir."

"And it was the widow, I presume, who was signaling for aid. Well, I'll stand by and see what's wanted. You'd better come back also."

"Aw, we don't want to," spoke Ted.

"No, I suppose not. Still you're coming."

The man had both boys firmly by their arms, and he turned in the gateway with them. As he did so, Mrs. Mooney, hearing voices, ventured to open her door. The light streamed out and showed the face of the man. At the sight of it Bob uttered an exclamation.

"Why, it's Captain Spark!" he cried.

"That's what. You read my signals right, my lad, and if I'm not mistaken, you're Bob Henderson."

"Yes, sir."

Captain Jeremiah Spark was an old seafaring man. He was a distant relative of Bob's mother, and, in fact, he was on his way to call on her, having just returned from a long voyage, when he ran into the boys, or, rather, they collided with him.

"So you're playing tricks on a poor, lone widow woman, are you?" asked the captain in no very pleasant tones.

"We—we didn't mean any harm," said Bob.

"No, I suppose not. Boys never do, but the harm comes. Now I'm going to march you two lads right up before the mast; and you're going to apologize to the widow. If you don't, why, I reckon a cat-o'-nine-tails will fit the case pretty well."

Mrs. Mooney was standing in her door as the captain led the two boys up to her.

"Here's the burglars you were shouting about, ma'am," he said. "One of 'em a relative of mine, I'm sorry to say. They've come to beg your pardon. Go ahead, boys."

"I'm sorry about the tic-tac," said Bob in a low voice.

"We didn't mean nothin'," added Ted.

"Was it you boys?" asked the widow. "I was so frightened. I thought burglars were trying to cut out a pane of glass."

"I don't believe they'll do it again," remarked Captain Spark. "Will you, boys?"

"No, sir," they chorused.

"That's right. Now come on, Bob. I'm going to your house."

The captain was warmly welcomed by Mr. and Mrs. Henderson a little later. Bob was wondering whether the captain would say anything about the recent prank, but the old seaman said nothing, though his eyes twinkled when, in response to a question from Mr. Henderson as to where the captain had met Bob, the former replied that there had been a collision in the dark.

That night, after Bob had gone to bed, Mrs. Henderson had a talk with her relative.

"I don't know what to do with Bob," she said. "He is always getting into mischief. He is not a bad boy at heart, but he is thoughtless."

"Yes, that he is," agreed Captain Spark.

"I am almost sure he was up to some prank tonight," went on Bob's mother. "I shall probably hear about it in the morning, when some of the neighbors call to make a complaint. Oh, dear, I wish I knew what to do!"

"I'll tell you what," suddenly exclaimed the captain, banging his fist down on the table with emphasis. "Let me take him to sea with me aboard the Eagle."

"Take him to sea? Take Bob on a voyage?" asked Mrs. Henderson.

"That's it! You let me take him, and I'll guarantee I'll make a man of him. The land is no place for a boy, anyhow. He needs a bit of ocean travel to broaden his views."

"That is a strange proposition," said Mr. Henderson. "We must think it over."

# CHAPTER IV

## TALKING IT OVER

Captain Spark was invited to spend a week or more at the Henderson home. He was up bright and early the next morning—in fact, before any one else, and Bob, hearing some one moving around downstairs, and knowing his father and mother were not in the habit of having such an early breakfast, descended to see who it was.

"Good-morning, my lad," greeted the mariner. "I suppose you are going to take the morning watch and holystone the decks. Nothing like being active when you're young. It will keep you from getting old."

"Yes, sir," replied Bob, for he did not know what else to say.

"Haven't got any more tic-tacs, have you?" and there was a twinkle in the captain's eyes.

"No, sir."

"That's right. If you've got to play tricks, do it on somebody your size. Then it's fair. Don't scare lone widows."

"I won't do it again," promised Bob, who felt a little ashamed of his prank of the previous night.

Soon Mrs. Henderson came downstairs to get breakfast, and

when the meal was over Bob got ready for school, Mr. Henderson leaving for his work in the woolen mill.

When Bob was safely out of the way Captain Spark once more brought up before Mrs. Henderson the proposition he had made the night before.

"Well, Lucy," he said, for he called Mrs. Henderson by her first name, "have you thought over what I said about taking Bob to sea?"

"Yes, I have."

"And what do you think of it?"

"Well, to tell you the truth, I don't like the idea."

"Why not? I'm sure it would be good for him."

"It might. I'm sure you mean it well, but I couldn't bear to have him go."

"It will make a man of him—cure him of some of his foolish ways, I'm sure."

"Perhaps it would. Bob is very wild, I know, but I think I have more influence over him than any one else. He will do anything for me, or for his father, either, for that matter. I am afraid if Bob got away from our influence he would be worse than he is now."

"Oh, we have a few good influences aboard the Eagle" said the captain with a grim smile. "Only we don't call 'em influences. We call 'em ropes' ends, or cat-o'-nine-tails, or a belaying-pin. I've known a limber rope's end, applied in the right place, do more good to a boy than lots of medicine."

"Oh, but, captain, I couldn't have Bob beaten!"

"No, of course not, I was only joking. Not that it doesn't do a boy good, though, once in a while, to have a good tanning. But I don't recommend it for a steady diet."

"Bob's father has never whipped him since he was a small lad," went on Mrs. Henderson. "Not that he doesn't seem to deserve it sometimes even now, but Mr. Henderson believes in talking to him and showing him how wrong he has acted."

"Yes, talk is good," admitted the mariner, "but if there's a rope's end handy, it sometimes makes the talk a little more effective—just a little bit."

"I suppose life aboard a sailing ship is very hard now-a-days," ventured Mrs. Henderson. Somehow she dwelt on the plan of having the captain take Bob, though she felt she could not consent to it.

"No harder than it ever was. In fact, it's easier than when I was a boy and ran away to sea. Those were hard days, and I've never forgot 'em. That's why I try to treat all my sailors and cabin boys as if they were human beings. Now you'd better think my plan over. It would do Bob a world of good to go to sea. You'd hardly know him when he got back."

"Oh, I don't know what to do," said Bob's mother. "No, I don't think I can consent. He might be drowned, and I would never forgive myself. I don't believe his father would consent either."

"Well, think it over," advised the captain. "I'm going to be in this port for some time. We're loading for a trip around Cape Horn, and it will take two weeks or more to get in shape. There's time enough to decide between now and then."

"I don't believe I could ever consent," declared Mrs. Henderson. "I think Bob will settle down pretty soon and give up playing pranks."

"I don't," said the captain to himself. "That boy is too full of mischief. He needs a sea voyage to soak some of it out of him. But that's the way with mothers. Well, I'll wait a while. I think something may happen to make her change her mind before I sail."

The captain did not know what a good prophet he was.

When Bob came home from school that noon-time he was surprised to see his mother and Captain Spark in earnest conversation. At first Bob thought the mariner might be telling of the escapade of the tic-tac, but when his mother made a warning gesture of silence to Captain Spark on beholding Bob the boy was puzzled.

"They must have been talking about me," he decided; "but what could it be? I don't think he would tell about the tic-tac, but there's certainly something queer afoot."

The truth was that the captain was renewing his plan of taking Bob to sea. Had the boy known of it he would have been much surprised, for he never dreamed of such a thing.

"How did you get along at school to-day?" asked Captain Spark, as Mrs. Henderson went out to get dinner.

"Pretty well."

"Didn't put any bent pins in the teacher's chair, did you?"

"No, sir."

The boy hoped the captain would not ask him what other prank he had been up to, for the truth was that Bob had that morning taken a live mouse to the classroom, releasing it during a study period, and nearly sending the woman teacher and the girl pupils into hysterics. His part had not been discovered, but the teacher had threatened to keep the whole class of boys in that night until the guilty one confessed, and

Bob knew he would have to tell sooner or later, if some of his companions did not "squeal" on him, in order that they might be released from suspicion.

"That's right," went on the mariner. "Never put bent pins in the teacher's chair."

As Bob feared, some one during the afternoon session told of his part in the mouse episode, and he was the only one kept in. The teacher made him stay while she corrected a lot of examination papers, and in the silent schoolroom the boy began to wish he had not been so fond of a "joke."

The teacher, who was a kind-hearted woman, talked seriously to her rather wild pupil, pointing out that it was a cowardly thing for a boy to frighten girls. Bob had never looked at it in just that light, and he was pretty well ashamed of himself when he was allowed to go home, with an admonition that he must mend his ways or be liable to expulsion.

"I'll bet he's been up to some mischief, Lucy," said Captain Spark when Bob came home quite late that afternoon.

"Perhaps he has. I hope it was nothing serious."

"Shall I ask him what it was?"

"No, we'll find it out sooner or later, and I don't want his father to worry more than he has to. He has hard work at the mill, and I like his evenings to be as free from care as possible."

"That's just like a woman," growled the mariner to himself. "They take more than their share of the burdens that the men and boys ought to bear. But never mind. I'll get Bob yet, and when I do I'll make a man of him or know the reason why. He'll find it much different on board ship from what he has it here in this quiet little village."

Bob was all unconscious of what fate had in store for him.

# CHAPTER V

## A JOKE THAT WENT WRONG

For several days after the prank with the mouse Bob did not play any jokes. The teacher ascribed that fact to the lecture she had given him. Bob's mother, who also noticed that he was much more quiet than usual, feared he was going to be sick.

"I never knew him to be so subdued," she thought. "I think I must give him some sulphur and molasses. Perhaps he is getting some disease."

She mentioned it to the captain.

"Nonsense," said the mariner. "He's hatching up some trick, that's what he's doing. You want to look out."

"Oh, captain, I don't think so!"

"Well, I do. Now you mark my words. It's down on the chart that Bob is up to some mischief. He's hauled down his colors for a while, but that's only to fool the enemy. First thing you know he'll hoist the Jolly Roger, and then there'll be some queer doings in these waters."

"Hoist the Jolly Roger?"

"I mean turn pirate, so to speak. You keep your eye on that

boy, Lucy. Something's going to break loose or I'm a Dutchman."

Bob's father thought his son's subdued behavior on the few days following the captain's arrival was due to a hint Bob had obtained, that, unless he mended his ways, he might be sent on a long voyage to work his passage.

Now the truth was that Bob was merely waiting for a good chance to play a trick. He was not particular what sort of a trick it was so long as it created a laugh. The consequences never gave him a thought or worry.

So, as he could think of nothing sufficiently "funny" to do, he remained quiet. But all the while he was looking about to see if he and his boon companion, Ted Neefus, could not perpetrate some prank that would be "worth while."

"Things are awful slow," complained Ted one afternoon as he and Bob walked home from school.

"That's right," agreed Bob. "But wait. I've got a plan."

"What is it?"

Bob looked carefully up and down the street. Then he glanced behind him. Next he drew Ted into some bushes that lined the thoroughfare on which they were walking.

"You know what's going to happen Friday night, don't you?" Bob asked.

"No; what?"

"The annual donation party for the minister."

"Well, what of it?"

"I'm going."

"That's nothing. Don't you generally go? So do I, though I don't see much fun in it. Ma makes me. She says it saves gittin' a meal at home, but I don't like the stuff they have there."

"I don't either—not much—but I'm going this time and so are you. Because, listen, something's going to happen."

"Honest?"

Bob nodded vigorously several times. There was a bright twinkle in his eyes.

"Don't say a word to anybody," he cautioned Ted, "but just you be on hand. This is going to be the best joke yet."

"Maybe he'll get mad."

"What if he does? He won't know who did it. You and I will be up in the gallery, or somewhere, and no one will see us. I'll bet there'll be some fun."

The chief trouble was, as I have pointed out before, that Bob's ideas of fun and those of other persons did not always agree. Boys and older folks seldom think the same on any subject, and so how can they be expected to about "jokes"?

The minister's donation party was an annual affair in More-ville. Rev. Daniel Blackton, who had charge of the only church in the village, did not receive a very large salary, and it was the custom to give him a "donation party" once a year to help pay him.

This usually took the form of a supper, held in the church parlors. The women of the congregation provided the food, and a small price was charged for the meal. Nearly every one, including the "men folks" and the children, attended, and sometimes quite a fair sum was realized in this way.

In addition, every one who could afford to was expected to

bring some "donation" for the minister. The women would knit him mittens, or slippers, or socks, they would crochet articles for the minister's wife, or bring jars of preserves, which were very welcome at the parsonage.

The men would donate wood, garden products, or whatever they could best afford. In this way, while the reverend gentleman's salary was not large, he managed to obtain a comfortable living.

It was to this donation party, or supper, that Bob and Ted were going, and as they crouched in the shadow of the bushes they perfected Bob's plan for some fun.

Mrs. Henderson was usually on the committee of arrangements for the supper, and this occasion was no exception. For a week before she was busy making pies and cakes and getting great pans of baked beans ready, for the supper victuals were of a plain but very wholesome sort.

As Captain Spark was a guest at the Henderson home at the time the supper was to be held, he, of course, was invited to attend, an invitation he quickly accepted, for he was fond of hearty eating, and he was not ashore often enough so that such affairs as donation suppers were distasteful to him, as they are to some persons.

At last the eventful evening came. Bob, dressed in his best suit, prepared to accompany his parents and Captain Spark to the church.

Such a thing as their son attempting a joke at the donation supper never occurred to Mr. or Mrs. Henderson. It is true that at the affair there was more or less jollity and good-natured fun after the formal function of supper was over and the minister had asked the blessing. But no one had ever dared play such a joke as Bob contemplated. If his mother had in the least suspected him of even dreaming of it she would have made him stay at home.

There was a good-sized throng in the church when the Henderson party arrived. Long tables had been set in the parlors, which were back of the church proper. Women in long white aprons were hurrying to and fro, getting ready to serve the meal. Bob followed his parents and the captain into the edifice.

"Is everything all ready?" asked Ted Neefus in a whisper as he approached Bob.

"Don't come near me," was the cautious answer. "Folks'll suspect if they see us together."

So Ted quickly glided away and was lost in the crowd.

The tables were all set, the victuals put on, and nearly every one had arrived.

"I guess we'd better get the chairs up now," proposed Mrs. Olney, who with Mrs. Henderson was superintending things. "Some of the boys can do it."

"I will, mom," volunteered Bob, who stood near his mother. "I'll get some of the fellows to help me."

"That's good," said Mrs. Henderson.

Bob hurried away, and soon he, Ted Neefus, Will Merton, Sam Shoop and some other chums were placing the chairs at the long tables.

"Is it all ready?" asked Ted in a hoarse whisper.

"Hush, can't you!" cautioned Bob. "Do you want to give it away?"

All was in readiness for the grown folks to sit down. They would eat first, then the tables would be set anew and the young people would have their turn. There was always more fun at the second table, and Bob and his chums would take their meals there.

Some one told Rev. Daniel Blackton that supper was ready, and he moved up to the head of the table, prepared to say grace. In honor of Mrs. Henderson, who was one of the chief workers in the church, her relative, Captain Spark, had been accorded a place next to the minister,

"Come on up in the gallery now," said Bob to Ted. "We can see the fun from there." Bob had been busy straightening the chairs near the head of the table.

Just as the boys reached the gallery, the assembled diners took their seats. The reverend gentleman stood up to say grace, and then sat down.

"How long before it works ?" asked Ted.

"It's working now," replied Bob, "but you won't see the full effect until he gets up."

"Think he'll make much of a fuss?"

"Naw. He's too good-natured. He'll only laugh."

The meal progressed. To and fro went the women with big plates of food. Every one seemed to have a good appetite, and some young people, who were hungry, began to think the grown folks would never get done.

But at last there was a general scraping of chairs as they were pushed back.

"Watch now!" called Bob to several of his cronies who were with him in the gallery that overlooked the room where supper was being served. "He's getting up."

In fact nearly every one was leaving the table. The tall form of

Frank V. Webster

Rev. Daniel Blackton was seen to rise. Something else arose also. It was the minister's chair. He felt that something was wrong, and half turned around. What he saw caused a deep flush to spread over his pale face.

His chair was glued fast to him, and wherever he moved the chair went too!

"Oh!" exclaimed Bob in a hoarse and horrified whisper. "I put the stuff on the wrong chair! I wanted Captain Spark to stick fast, and I put it on the minister's chair by mistake!"

By this time the dominie was endeavoring to pull the chair loose from the seat of his trousers. But the glue Bob had spread was very sticky. Pull and tug as he did, the minister could not free himself.

First there was a murmur, then some one laughed. In a moment the whole room was in an uproar.

"You'll catch it!" prophesied Ted, in an awestruck whisper.

"I won't unless some of you squeal on me," declared Bob.

He looked over the balcony railing at the struggling minister, who was trying in vain to get free from the chair.

"Nobody'll squeal," declared Will Merton.

"Of course not," added Sam Shoop.

# CHAPTER VI

## MRS. HENDERSON'S DECISION

The minister, very much embarrassed, was doing his best to get rid of the chair. It was hard work, for if he turned around to one side to grasp it, the chair, naturally, swung away from him. It was several seconds before any one thought to aid him. Then Captain Spark came to his relief.

"Guess I'll have to give you a hand, dominie," he said. "You're anchored pretty hard and fast on a shoal, and you'll need help to break loose. How did it happen? Did you sit down on an egg?"

"Some one put glue in the chair. I did not notice it until I tried to get up."

"Glue, eh?"

The captain's eyes had a queer look in them.

"Yes. I suppose some of the boys did it for a joke."

"Pretty poor sort of a joke," remarked Mrs. Olney. "I could almost put my hand on the boy that did it, too."

She looked to see if Mrs. Henderson had heard her, but Bob's mother was on the other side of the room and was not fully aware of what had happened.

Frank V. Webster

Captain Spark tried to pull the chair loose from the minister, but the glue had taken a firm hold, and the only result of his efforts was to drag the reverend gentleman about the room.

All this while the people were trying hard not to laugh. But it was impossible. Men were chuckling and endeavoring to suppress their mirth, and nearly all the women were red in the face from holding in their laughter.

"Guess you'd better sit down, dominie," advised the captain.

"If I do, I'll stick faster than before."

"Well, if you do I'll put my feet on the rounds of the chair and hold it down while you get up. Maybe you can pull loose."

"I'm afraid," said Rev. Mr. Blackton.

"Afraid of what?"

"I might tear my trousers, and," he added in a whisper to the captain, "they're the best pair I have."

"Might as well be killed for a sheep as a goat," replied the mariner. "They're spoiled anyhow, by this glue. Better try to pull loose. Go on. I'll hold your chair down."

Thus advised, the minister sat down. The crowd watched with anxiety, not unmixed with mirth. Even the clergyman himself could not help smiling, though it was quite an embarrassing position for a dignified gentleman.

"Would you mind putting your feet on the rounds on the other side?" asked the captain of Mr. Henderson. "Between us both I guess we can hold him down."

The two men bore heavily on the chair-rounds, and Mr. Blackton strained to rise. There was a pulling, ripping sound, and he hesitated. Then, feeling that he must get loose no matter what happened, he gave a mighty tug and was free. But his trousers, though only slightly torn, were covered with glue.

Now that it was over, and the excitement was beginning to cool down, the minister began to feel a little natural anger at the perpetrator of the "Joke." His best trousers were spoiled, and the donation supper had been thrown into confusion.

"Who did it?" was the question asked on every side.

The boys came slowly down from the gallery and mingled unnoticed with the throng. Bob was a little worried. He had not meant to humiliate the minister, but had counted on Captain Spark getting stuck to the chair. The captain, he knew, would make light of the prank. But it was no small matter to have done this thing to the clergyman.

"Going to supper?" asked Ted of Bob.

"No. I don't feel like eating. Guess I'll go home."

But Bob's plan was frustrated. His mother, who had been looking for her son, caught sight of him.

"Oh, Bob!" she exclaimed. "I hope none of the boys that you go with played that horrid trick on the minister! It was a very mean thing to do! But you had better have your supper. The table will soon be ready again."

Bob did not have much appetite. He was afraid of being discovered.

The chair, with the glue on it, had been taken to the cellar, and the minister had gone home to change his trousers. Captain Spark, who had begun to turn certain things over in his mind, approached Bob. He had a sharp eye, had the mariner, and, in looking closely at his relative's son, he saw a bit of evidence that Bob had not counted on. This was nothing more nor less than a big spot of glue on the lad's coat sleeve.

Frank V. Webster

"What's this?" asked the seaman, pointing to the sticky place.

"I don't know. Glue—I guess," replied Bob, turning pale.

"Glue, eh? Seems to be about as sticky as that on the minister's chair."

At the mention of glue several persons about Bob and the captain looked curiously at them. Mrs. Henderson, who was just then passing, carrying a big platter of baked beans, stopped to listen to what the seaman was saying.

"Yes, it's glue," remarked the mariner. "Just like that on the chair. Bob," he asked suddenly, "did you put that glue there?"

Now, with all his faults, Bob would never tell a lie. He regarded that as cowardly, and he was always willing to take whatever punishment was coming to him for his "jokes."

"Yes, captain," he said in a low voice. "I did it."

"Ha! I thought so."

"Bob Henderson!" exclaimed his mother, her face flushing red with mortification. "Did you play that horrid joke on the minister?"

"Yes, but I didn't mean to."

"You didn't mean to?"

"No. I thought some one else was going to sit on that chair."

"You thought some one else was? Why, that's just as bad—almost. Who did you think would sit there?"

"Captain Spark!"

"You young rascal!" exclaimed the commander of the *Eagle*,

but he did not seem very angry. "So that was intended to anchor me down, eh? Well, I must look into this."

"I thought you'd sit there," went on Bob.

"So I was going to, but the minister made me change, as he's a little deaf on one side, and he wanted to ask me some questions about the Fiji Islanders."

There was now quite a crowd around Bob, his mother, and the captain. Mrs. Henderson did not know what to do. Up to now Bob's pranks had been bad enough, but to play this trick on the minister, and at the annual donation supper, where nearly every person in the village was present, was the climax. She felt that she had been much humiliated.

Bob's father heard what had happened, and came up to his son.

"Bob," he said, in a curiously quiet voice, "you must go home at once. I shall have to punish you severely for this."

Bob knew what that meant. He wished, most heartily, that he had not played this last prank. But it was too late now.

"I told you I thought he was up to something," whispered the captain to Mrs. Henderson.

"Yes, you were right," she admitted. "Now my mind is made up. Captain, I wish you would take him to sea with you at once! I can stand his foolishness no longer!"

Bob was out of the room by this time and did not hear his mother's decision.

"Do you mean that, Lucy?" asked Captain Spark eagerly.

"Yes, I do. I am determined. Bob shall go to sea. Perhaps it will teach him a lesson, and he will mend his ways."

"It will be the making of him," declared the captain heartily. "I'm glad you decided this. I'll make arrangements at once."

# CHAPTER VII

## BOB IS DELIGHTED

The excitement caused by Bob's prank had somewhat quieted down, and the preparations went on for giving the young people their supper. Several of Bob's chums, however, fearful that they might be suspected of having taken part in the trick, left the church.

As a matter of fact, though, Bob alone was concerned. He had thought of the trick, procured a bottle of liquid glue from the drug store, and, watching his chance, had poured it on the chair. Then he had told his chums of it, and they had withdrawn with him to the gallery to watch events, which came quickly enough.

At the supper-table of the young people, little was talked of but Bob's prank, and opinion was pretty evenly divided as to what would happen.

"Maybe the minister will have him arrested," suggested one girl.

"Oh, I don't think so," was the opinion of another. "Mr. Blackton is a kind-hearted man, and he likes Bob."

"But I don't believe he'll like him after tonight."

"Maybe not. It was a mean thing to do, but I couldn't help

laughing when the minister stood up and the chair went with him, swinging around every time he moved, the legs hitting everybody."

"Yes, it was odd. I had to laugh, too."

The girls and several of their companions indulged in merriment at the recollection. The minister soon returned to the church parlors, wearing a different pair of trousers, and he seemed to have regained his good humor.

"Who was the boy who wanted me to remain seated all the evening, and perhaps longer?" he asked.

"It was Bob Henderson," volunteered several.

"Yes, Mr. Blackton," said Mrs. Henderson. "I am sorry to have to admit that it was my son who played that prank. But he is going to be punished for it. His father has sent him home and has followed after him."

"I hope he will not punish Bob too severely. It was a boyish prank, due more to thoughtlessness than to malice."

"I suppose it was, but Bob plays altogether too many such pranks. I think this will be the last."

"Well, tell Bob I forgive him, though my trousers are ruined."

"Mr. Henderson will arrange with you about that."

"What—er—what chastisement does he contemplate administering to Bob?" asked the minister. He and Mrs. Henderson were conversing off to one side, in a corner of the room. "I hope he will not whip him. Bob is too big a boy to be whipped."

"Still, parson, you know what the Good Book says: 'Spare the rod and spoil the child.'"

"Yes, Mrs. Henderson, I know. Chastisement is all right in many cases, but there are other means."

"And it is my plan to take them," went on Bob's mother. "I have just made arrangements with Captain Spark to take Bob with him on a long sea voyage."

"A sea voyage? That ought to be fine. Yes, I think that will be better than whipping Bob. Tell your husband I said so."

"I shall. Now, if you will excuse me, I must see that these young people have plenty to eat. They are a hungry lot."

"Indeed they are. Don't forget to tell Bob I forgive him. I don't want him to worry. Tell him, also, that he must be a little more thoughtful."

"I will."

When Captain Spark and Mrs. Henderson went home from the donation supper that night they discussed on the way the further plans of sending Bob to sea.

"We must consult Mr. Henderson about it," said the captain.

"I shall, this very night. I will put up with Bob's nonsense no longer."

Mr. Henderson was found sitting in the dining-room, reading a paper. He had sent Bob to bed on arriving at the house, for Mr. Henderson was a man who did not believe in inflicting punishment in the heat of passion. He wanted to calm down before he decided how his son ought to be made to realize the wrong he had done. To tell the truth, he was quite at a loss just what punishment to inflict.

He had thought of a sound whipping, but he realized, as had the minister, that Bob was too old for this. Nothing so breaks the proud spirit of a boy as personal chastisement, after he has reached a certain age.

And, as yet, Mr. Henderson was not aware of the proposition Captain Spark had made to Bob's mother, and her practical acceptance of it. Of course, Mr. Henderson had heard the first talk of sending Bob to sea, but after his wife's refusal to consider it he had thought no more about it.

"Well, Enos," asked Mrs. Henderson, as she and the captain entered, "have you considered what to do with Bob?"

"I have, Lucy, but I have reached no conclusion."

"I have."

"You have? What is it?"

"I am going to send him on a voyage with Captain Spark. That is, if you consent."

"I will agree to anything you think best. But I think you will find it hard work to get Bob to go. I fear he will dislike the idea very much."

"Why so?" inquired the captain.

"Well, Bob has many friends in the village—many boy-chums —and I think he would object very strongly to leaving them, and going off among a lot of strange men in a ship."

"I wouldn't be a stranger to him."

"No, you would not, but the others would be. And I think he would be somewhat afraid."

"Afraid? What's there to be afraid of on the ocean, with a stout deck beneath your feet? The ocean is the safest place in the world. I'm frightened half out of my wits every time I come on land. There are so many chances of accidents. The train may run off the track, steam-boilers may blow up, there may be an earthquake, a wild bull may chase you, you may fall down a coal-hole and break your neck, or a building may topple over on you while you're walking peacefully along the street. No such things as those can happen to you on the ocean."

"No, perhaps not, but there are others as bad, or worse, captain."

"Nonsense! It may blow a bit, now and then, but all you've got to do is mind your helm and you'll come out all right."

"I am glad you think so. I should be very glad to have Bob make a trip with you. I think it would do him good, but I fear he will object to it."

"I don't think so. We'll propose it to him in the morning."

Bob came down to breakfast feeling rather sheepish. He had been wondering, during the time he was not sleeping, what form of punishment his father would inflict.

The lad had an uneasy feeling that he might have to make a public apology before the whole church congregation. This he felt would be very embarrassing. He also had an idea that his father might take him from school and put him to work in the mill. Mr. Henderson had once threatened this when Bob had played some particularly annoying prank. And Bob liked his school very much, in spite of the tricks he played,

"Well, my son," said Mr. Henderson, more solemnly than he usually spoke, "I trust you have a proper feeling of regret for what you did last night."

"Yes. I wish I hadn't done it," said Bob. "I didn't think it would make so much trouble. I didn't mean to use so much glue."

"Well, there is no use in discussing that now. The thing is

done. You remember I told you I would have to punish you?"

"Yes, sir."

"I have talked it over with your mother and Captain Spark, and we have made up our minds what to do. You are going to be sent on a long sea voyage with Captain Spark, in the *Eagle*. You will be away from home a long time, and, when you return, I trust you will have mended your ways."

For a few seconds Bob did not speak. The proposition was so sudden to him that he did not exactly comprehend it.

"I'm to go to sea with Captain Spark?" he asked slowly.

"That is the punishment we have decided on, my son."

"Where are you going, captain?" asked Bob.

"I'm bound for 'round Cape Horn this trip. Oh, you'll get all the ocean you want, but it will make a man of you."

"When are you going to sail?" asked Bob in a quiet voice.

"Next week."

"Good!" exclaimed the youth suddenly. "I'll be ready. Oh, I always wanted to make a sea voyage, and now I have the chance. This is the best ever! Hurrah! That's the stuff! 'A life on, the ocean wave, a home on the bounding deep!' Avast and belay, my hearties! Shiver my timbers! All hands on deck to take in sail! There she blows!"

Bob had not read sea stories for nothing.

"That's the way to talk!" exclaimed the captain. "I knew he'd like the idea!"

Mr. Henderson seemed somewhat amazed. He had expected

Bob to make strong objections. Instead the boy was delighted.

"I am sorry to see you leave home, Bob," said his mother, with just the hint of tears in her eyes, "but I think it will be the best thing for you."

"So do I, mom. Hurrah! This is the best ever!"

Then Bob began to dance a sailor's hornpipe.

"It seems to me," said Mr. Henderson to himself, as he started for the mill, "that Bob's punishment is more of a pleasure than anything else. Still, if it does him good, I'll not regret it."

# CHAPTER VIII

## GETTING READY

Captain Spark's ship, the *Eagle*, was a large craft, and in her he had made many voyages. At present the vessel was docked at a seaport town not many miles from Moreville.

The day it was announced to Bob that he was to make a sea voyage, the captain left the village to visit the *Eagle* at the dock and see how the loading of the cargo was progressing.

"I want to sail as soon as possible," he said, "and though I left a good mate in charge, still I like to look after certain matters myself. I'll be back in a few days and let you know, Bob, the exact date for sailing. In the meanwhile you can be getting ready."

"Aye, aye, sir," answered the boy, trying, as he had read of sailors doing, to pull a lock of his reddish hair, but finding it too short. He had decided to adopt all the sea practices he had ever read about.

"Get your bag ready," went on the captain, "have your mother put some needles and thread in, for you'll have to mend your own clothes at sea, and I'll look it over when I get back."

"Aye, aye, sir."

The captain laughed at Bob's sudden enthusiasm for the sea

and ship terms, but he was not displeased.

As for Bob, he thought the time would never pass until he would find himself aboard the *Eagle*. That very day he began to sort over his clothes, trying to decide which he should take, and he had such a miscellaneous collection of garments that, when his mother saw them, she laughed.

"Bob!" she exclaimed. "It would take three trunks to hold them, and I don't believe sailors are ever allowed more than one. At least, in all the pictures I ever saw of sailors going on board a ship they only had a small box or bag on their shoulder, and, of course, that must have contained all their clothes."

"I guess you're right, mother. I'll have to sort out some of these."

"Never mind. I'll do that. But what in the world are you doing with those rubber boots?"

"I was going to take them along."

"Sailors seldom wear rubber boots. They go barefoot when it's wet on deck." For Mrs. Henderson knew something about seafaring men, from her long acquaintance with Captain Spark.

"Another mistake," admitted Bob, good-naturedly. "Guess I've got lots to learn about the ocean and ships."

"Yes indeed, Bob. And I hope you will profit by it. It is no place to play pranks, either, on board a ship."

"But I've read that when the ship crosses the equator the sailors cut up all kinds of high jinks."

"Yes, I suppose they do, but that is not very often. I have no doubt Captain Spark will permit fun on that occasion."

"If we go down around Cape Horn and up the west coast of North and South America we'll cross the equator twice," went on Bob. "We can have fun both times."

"I'm afraid you're thinking more of the fun you are going to have than the real reason for this voyage, Bob. It is a punishment for your prank on the minister."

"I know it, but, mom, I can't seem to feel that way about it."

"And I don't know as I blame you, Bob, though of course it was very wrong to put glue on the reverend gentleman's chair."

Bob felt he must tell the news of his prospective voyage to his chums. Leaving his mother to sort out his clothes, he went out in the street. It was Saturday and there was no school. In fact, the term would close in another week, so Bob would miss little instruction by taking the cruise.

The first lad Bob met was Ted Neefus. His chum hurried up to him and Inquired:

"Did he hurt you very much?"

"Who?"

"Your father."

"My father? What do you mean?"

"Didn't he give you a good walloping for that joke?"

"No. Not a bit of it. I'm going on a sea voyage with Captain Spark."

"Honest?"

"Cross my heart," and Bob went through a rapid motion with his hands somewhere over the region of his stomach.

"Where to?"

"Around Cape Horn."

"No jokin'?"

"Of course not. But that's nothing. Captain Spark has been all over the world."

Bob spoke as though doubling the Horn was the easiest thing a mariner meets with.

"I wonder if he doesn't want another boy," mused Ted wistfully.

"Don't believe so."

"Wish he did. We could have jolly times together."

"I'm going out to learn how to sail a ship, not to have fun," replied Bob, with an air of lofty virtue. He had said nothing about this voyage being a sort of discipline as punishment for his prank. He did not think that necessary.

"When are you goin'?"

"Next week." And then the two boys fell to discussing the trip in all its aspects. Soon other boys joined Bob and Ted, but the perpetrator of the glue-joke was the center of attraction.

In fact, Bob was regarded as a sort of village hero. There was more interest manifested in geography at school the following week than ever before. Everybody knew, without telling, where Cape Horn was, and as for the Straits of Magellan, they could have pointed them out in the dark.

The prospect of the trip, too, had a certain effect on Bob. His mind was so filled with the thought of it, that he actually forgot about planning any jokes. Nor would he take part in

Frank V. Webster

any with the other village boys.

"Let's go down past old Mary Bounder's house and throw stones at the door. Then she'll come out and chase us and one of us can go in and get her pet cat and tie a can to its tail," proposed Ted the following Monday. Mary Bounder was a curious old woman, who lived all alone in a cabin near the woods, and was the mark for many a joke on the part of the boys.

"Nope," said Bob firmly.

"What's the matter? Sick?" asked Ted in surprise.

"No, but I've got to do some studying."

"Studying? Why, there's only a little more school."

"I don't mean that kind of studying. I'm learning the different parts of a ship, so I'll know 'em when I get to sea."

Ted had momentarily forgotten about Bob's voyage.

"That's so," he said. "You'll be going away soon. Say, we ought to have some fun before you go."

"Guess I've played enough jokes for a while."

"But we ought to have one more. Come down to Mary Bounder's. Sam Shoop will go. He'll catch the cat."

"Nope. I'm going home. I got a new book on sea terms, and I want to look at it."

"All right. Then Sam and I'll go. You'll wish you'd come. We'll have some fun."

But Bob could not be persuaded. His mother and father noticed the change in him, and they were delighted.

"I believe we made no mistake when we consented to the captain's plan," said Mr. Henderson.

"If it will only last," added his wife.

That day a letter came from Captain Spark saying he would be detained a few days longer and would not reach Moreville until Wednesday.

"The ship will sail the following Saturday," he stated in his note. "I could sail Friday, but I don't want to take any chances. Some of my sailors are superstitious, and I want them all to be in good humor. I trust Bob has not changed his mind about going."

"No indeed," said the boy, when the letter was shown to him.

That afternoon as Bob was coming back from the store, he met, on the main street of the village, an old man who lived on the outskirts of the town. His name was Captain Obediah Hickson and he had once been a sailor, though he told so many different versions of his life at sea, that it was hard to say where truth began and fiction left off. Still he might not have meant to deceive any one, for he was rather simple-minded.

"What's this I hear about you going to take a long sea voyage?" he asked of Bob.

"It's true, Captain Obed," which was what every one called the aged man. "I'm going around Cape Horn with Captain Spark. We start soon."

"Around Cape Horn, eh? Then you'll strike the Southern Pacific."

"I expect so."

A curious change seemed to come over the old man. He looked carefully up and down the street to see that no one was

Frank V. Webster

in sight, and then, approaching quite closely to Bob, he whispered:

"Bob, come to my house to-night."

"What for?"

"Hush! Not so loud. I've a great secret to disclose."

"What about?" asked Bob with a smile, thinking to humor the old captain.

"About buried treasure. It's on a lonely island in the Southern Pacific Ocean. I'm the only living man who knows where it is. If I wasn't so old I'd go along and help find it. But I'm too old. It needs some one young and strong. You'll dig it up for me, won't you?"

"If I could find it," replied Bob, believing the aged man was speaking of some delusion.

"Oh, you can find it. I have the secret map. I'll give it to you. Come to my house to-night, but after dark—after dark, mind." And, once more looking around to see that no one had observed him, Captain Obed shuffled on down the street. Bob did not know what to think.

# CHAPTER IX

## BOB'S LAST LAND JOKE

Returning home, Bob said nothing to his mother about what Captain Obed had said. The boy wanted to think more about it. If he could combine a treasure hunt with his sea voyage it would be a fine thing. Besides, why should not the old man know something of hidden treasure? He had sailed in many waters and been on many ships. Bob decided he would visit him that night.

Accordingly, when it grew dusk, he set off for the lonely house where the old sailor lived. It was quite a walk, but in his eagerness Bob covered the ground in short time. As he was passing a clump of bushes, not far from his destination, he was surprised to hear a voice calling sharply from the darkness:

"Avast there!"

"Who is it?" asked Bob.

"It's me," replied Captain Obed in his husky voice. "I hid out here to signal you so's you wouldn't be followed."

"Followed? Who by?"

"By persons anxious to get hold of the secret map that tells of the treasure buried on the island. Are you all alone, Bob?"

"Of course."

"Then go ahead into my house. I'll follow as soon as I've taken an observation."

The boy thought the old man must be rather queer to imagine any one would try to steal his secret, if secret he had. Bob was half inclined to give the whole thing up. But he walked on, and was soon inside the rather humble home of the retired mariner. Presently Captain Obed entered and quickly closed the door.

"Have to be very careful—very careful," he said in a whisper. "If any one knowed I had this map they'd rob me of it."

He pulled down the shades of the windows, and then carefully locking the door he went to another room. Bob heard him fumbling about, and soon the old man came out with a yellowish piece of paper in his hand.

"Feel of it," he said to Bob.

Bob did so. It was stiff and crackly.

"Parchment—parchment," whispered Captain Obed. "The map is drawed on parchment—that's sheepskin instead of paper. He wanted it to last for years and years."

"Who did?"

Once more Captain Obed looked around to see if by chance any one had stolen into the room. He made Bob rather nervous.

"Captain Kidd," he answered in a lower whisper than he had yet used. "Captain Kidd drawed that map. It gives the real secret of his buried treasure. I'm the only one that knows where it is. There's lots of maps of Captain Kidd's treasure, but I've got the only real one. All them others was jest drawed so as to fool folks. An' they did fool 'em. 'Cause why? 'Cause nobody ain't never yet found the captain's treasure. But you'll find it, an' you'll bring it home to Captain Obed, won't you, Bob? Of course you will. You're a good boy, and if you bring it home safe, why, I'll give you"—he paused and seemed to make a great effort—"yes, I'll give you a hundred dollars, or maybe a hundred and fifty. There! What do you say to that?"

"How much treasure is there?" asked Bob, hardly knowing whether to laugh at the old man or take him seriously.

"How much? It must be near a million dollars. O h, there's lots of treasure!"

It struck Bob that if there was that amount he would not be getting much for his share.

"Now you take that map," went on Captain Obed. "It gives the exact location or the island, and shows where the treasure is buried on it, right in the center of a place where four trees grow. The island is about eighty-two degrees west longitude and twenty-one degrees south latitude. It'll be easy to locate. Just cruise about in that locality for a few days and you'll find it. Then dig up the treasure."

"But suppose Captain Spark doesn't want to cruise around there? It's his ship."

"Oh, you give him twenty-five dollars or so—out of your share, mind you—and he'll be glad enough to do it. Now, Bob, I rely on you. You're the only one I ever told my secret to, and I want you to keep it close. Don't let 'em get that map away from you. They'll try—oh, they'll try dreadful hard. I got it from my grandfather, who had it direct from Captain Kidd himself, so I know it's correct. Now, Bob, you'd better go. Take good care of the map and bring me the treasure."

He thrust the yellow, crackling piece of parchment into Bob's hands and opened the door.

Frank V. Webster

"Put it in your pocket," he cautioned as Bob went out. "Some one might see you."

Now Bob was quite a level-headed youth, and though he knew that sometimes treasure might be found on islands in the ocean, where it had been hidden by modern pirates or illegal pearl fishers, he did not take much stock in what Captain Obed had told him.

Still he thought it would be no harm to take the parchment and show it to Captain Spark. That seasoned mariner would soon be able to tell if it was worth anything. At any rate, Bob was not going to lie awake at night over the possibility—the very small possibility—of securing the treasure.

"Guess I'll have to make a better bargain for my share of it before I do much searching," he decided.

The boy said nothing to his parents about the parchment map. He preferred letting Captain Spark know of it first, as that seemed fairer to the old sailor who had given it to him. Then, as the time was drawing nearer to the date of sailing, Bob's thoughts dwelt more and more on his prospective trip.

"Don't you notice quite a change in Bob?" asked Mrs. Henderson of her husband the next day. "He seems to have settled down, and he hasn't played a joke in a long time."

"No, he hasn't. But you know the proverb about a new broom sweeping clean. Just now Bob's mind is so full of the sea that he thinks of nothing else. Wait a while. If he gets away with Captain Spark without playing some sort of a trick before he goes I'll be agreeably disappointed."

"I think he will. I'm so glad the captain came to pay us a visit when he did. It was a lucky thing for Bob."

"I think it was. He was getting quite reckless in his pranks."

The subject of this conversation was, of course, not aware of it. The truth was that Bob was fairly holding himself in. He saw many opportunities to play jokes—more, in fact, than he had ever seen before. It was a great temptation to indulge in pranks, but he reflected that if he got into any more trouble he might not be allowed to take the sea voyage.

"And I wouldn't want that to happen for the world," he said to himself. "Still I know a couple of dandy jokes I could play before I go. Maybe I might get Ted Neefus to do 'em, but I don't believe he could do 'em as good as I can."

Bob was pondering over the rather queer fact to him that old folks don't care half as much for jokes as boys do, when his mother asked him to go on an errand for her. This was to take a message to Mrs. Dodson, who lived in a large house on a hill just outside the village. She was quite wealthy, and Mrs. Henderson used to do some fine embroidering for her.

Bob, who was always ready to oblige his mother, took the package of sewing and the note which went with it and started off. On the way he passed the wagon of a certain old crusty farmer he knew. The vehicle was in front of a house where the farmer had gone to sell some butter and eggs. Dangling from the back of the wagon was a long rope, and it was a great temptation to Bob to take the rope and tie one of the rear wheels so that It would not revolve. The farmer, coming out in a hurry, would not notice it, and would wonder what was the matter when he started to drive off.

"But I guess I'd better not," thought Bob with a sigh. "He'd be sure to tell dad, and then I'd be in more trouble. I've got a pretty good reputation since the donation supper, and I don't want to spoil it."

Bob delivered the embroidery and note to Mrs. Dodson, and was on his way back home when he saw Susan Skipper, Mrs. Dodson's hired girl, and Dent Freeman, the hired man of the place, washing the big front windows of the house—that is,

Dent was washing them, perched upon a step-ladder, for Susan was quite heavy and was afraid to trust herself very high in the air. However, she was doing her share by handing up pails of warm water to Dent.

Now Dent and Susan, as Bob well knew, were what the country people call "sweet" on one another. Susan was very fond of the hired man, and as for Dent, he thought there never had been a better cook than Susan. They lost no chance of talking to each other, and as the window-cleaning operations afforded them a good opportunity, they were taking advantage of it.

All at once a daring plan came into Bob's mind. It seemed as if he could not resist it, for he thought of what he considered a fine "joke."

As he was well acquainted with the hired man and cook he walked toward them. Perhaps he would not have been flattered if he had heard what they said as he approached.

"Here comes that Henderson lad," remarked Dent. "He's allers up to some trick. Look out for him, Susan."

"Oh, I can look out for myself. It's you that wants to be cautious. He'd just like to spill your pail of water."

So they did not look with much favor on Bob's appearance. However, Bob, once he had set his mind on a bit of mischief, knew how to carry it through.

"Hello, Dent," he said good-naturedly. "Dad wants to know if you have any more of that rheumatic medicine you made. It fixed him up in great shape."

This was true enough, though Mr. Henderson had not given the message to Bob that day, having some time previously requested him to deliver it the first chance he got.

"Sure I have some more," replied the hired man. If he was open to flattery on any point, it was on his skill as a maker of rheumatism cures. He had tried several, and had at last decided that he had hit on one that was infallible. He had a notion of setting up in the drug business. "I'll get you a bottle if you wait a while, Bob," he said.

"I'll wait."

This was not very welcome news to Susan. She wanted to have a private conversation with Dent, and she could not while Bob was present. But the boy's plan was not completed.

As he stood idly by the step-ladder, on the top of which was Dent washing away at the windows, with the pail of warm water beside him, Bob appeared to be toying with a bit of string.

"I don't s'pose you have any doughnuts left, Susan?" he ventured rather wistfully.

Now Susan bad not forgiven Bob for a little joke he had played on her some time before, so at his hint, to show her displeasure, she turned her back and did not answer. This was Just what Bob wanted.

Looking up to see that Dent was not observing him, he passed one end of the string about the step-ladder. Tying it securely, he fastened the other end to Susan's apron strings in such a manner that it would not pull off.

"I'll wait for you out in the barn," he said to Dent when it became evident that Susan was not going to take the hint and get the doughnuts. In fact, Bob, much as he liked them, would have been disappointed if she had gone in for some. He wanted to get out of the way before a certain thing happened.

He strolled off, but instead of going to the barn he hid around the corner of the house. Susan and Dent conversed for several minutes longer, the man meanwhile busy at the windows. Then the cook, hearing her mistress calling her, started for the house in a hurry.

The result was disastrous. As she started off the string tied to the ladder and her apron tightened. As Susan was a woman of heavy weight, it did not take much effort on her part to pull over the ladder, together with Dent and the pail of water.

Dent came down to the ground, fortunately landing on his feet like a cat. The pail of water described a graceful curve and splashed on both Susan and the man. The cook, whose feet became tangled up in the falling ladder, slipped and fell, knocking Dent down, and there they were in a heap, both soaking wet.

And that was Bob's "joke." Hidden around the corner of the house, he laughed so he almost betrayed his position.

"Oh, that's too funny!" he whispered. "It was like clowns in a circus!"

# CHAPTER X

## OFF ON THE TRIP

For a few seconds both the cook and the hired man, whose feet Susan had knocked from under him, did not move. The suddenness of it all was too much for them. Then Dent arose after a struggle.

"Did you do that on purpose?" he asked Susan, an angry look coming over his face.

"Do what on purpose? What do you mean?"

"Did you upset my ladder?"

"Upset your ladder? Well, I guess not! But I'd like to know why you tried to throw that pail of water over me. If it was meant for a joke, I think it was a pretty poor one."

The woman started to arise, but found herself somewhat tangled up in the cord and ladder.

"Throw water on you?" repeated Dent with a puzzled look. "I didn't throw any water. It got on me as much as it did on you."

This was as near to a quarrel as these two had ever approached. Bob, listening around the corner of the house, was holding his sides to keep from bursting into laughter, though my own opinion is that he should have felt sorry for his "joke." It might have resulted disastrously, for either Susan or the hired man might have broken a leg or an arm. But Bob never thought of that. His sole idea was to create a laugh for himself.

Dent and Susan, dripping wet, looked at each other. Then the cook, wiping some of the water from her face, got up. As she did so the cord tied to her apron strings became tightened, and as Dent was partly standing on the step-ladder, Susan's progress was suddenly stopped.

"There!" she exclaimed, "That's what did it. My apron string got tangled in the ladder."

Dent examined the cord.

"No, it didn't get tangled," he announced. "It was tied there by some one, and I know who did it."

"Who?"

"Bob Henderson. Wait till I catch him! He did this for a joke. The young rascal! pretending he wanted some rheumatism medicine for his father! I'll fix him!"

Bob thought it was time to be moving on. He did not like the tone of Dent's voice.

But if the boy hoped to get off unseen he was disappointed. As he started to run he slipped and fell. Dent heard the noise the lad made, and while Susan was loosening the cord from her apron the man ran forward.

Bob, however, was up like a flash and ran off, but not before Dent had nearly caught him. Then the hired man knew it would be of no use to chase the mischievous lad, as Bob was very fleet of foot.

"You wait!" cried Dent, shaking his fist at Bob. "I'll fix you!"

"You can't!" was the answer. "I'm going on a voyage!"

"I hope you never come back here!" said Dent angrily. "I hope you get lost on a desert island where there's nothing to eat but seaweed!"

"That would serve him right," added the cook "The idea of hinting for some of my doughnuts! I'll tell his mother on him."

"And I'll tell his father," added Dent.

Bob was a little afraid lest Mrs. Dodson might come out, and seeing the state her employees were in, would know the lad had had a hand in it. The effects might be more unpleasant than they now promised to be. So Bob hastened his pace, and was soon out of sight of the big house on the hill. He left behind him two very angry persons, yet when they glanced at each other neither Susan nor Dent could help laughing. They looked as if they had been through a cyclone and cloud-burst, both at the same time, as the hired man expressed it.

Bob's father did hear of the trick, but not in the way the lad expected he would. On cooling down neither the hired man nor the cook felt like going and making a complaint about what Bob had done. The trick, however, had been witnessed by the coachman, and he told some friends in the village. In this way it became known to several persons, and Mr. Henderson heard of it.

"Bob," he said to his son very sternly that night, "I thought you had given up such foolishness as playing those tricks."

"I thought I had, too, dad, but I couldn't help doing this. Her apron strings came just in the right place."

"Do you think it was a nice thing to do?"

"No, sir. I s'pose not."

Mr. Henderson sighed. Bob was so frank to acknowledge a fault that it was hard to punish him.

"I don't know what's going to become of you," he said.

"Well, that was my last land joke, dad."

"Your last land joke? What do you mean?"

"I'm going to sail with Captain Spark soon, and I'll not have time for any more."

"That's so, and I'm glad of it. If you try any jokes on the sailors you may find they know a trick or two themselves."

"Oh, I'm going to turn over a new leaf."

"It's about time."

Bob really intended to mend his ways. This, perhaps, was due as much to a fear of what the sailors on the ship might do to him if he played any pranks on them as it was to a desire to reform.

That same night Captain Spark arrived at the Henderson home a little ahead of time. He announced that his ship was ready to sail, and that he and Bob would depart the next morning for the seaport town.

"All ready, Bob?" he asked.

"Aye, aye, sir."

"That's the way to talk. We may have to lay at the dock for a couple of days longer than I calculated on, but that will give you a chance to get acquainted with the ship before we strike blue water."

"That will be good."

With the return of the captain, Bob's visions of a life on the ocean wave were redoubled.

Mrs. Henderson cried a little when it came time to part the next morning, and there was a suspicious dampness in the eyes of Mr. Henderson. Bob also, in spite of the happy life he thought lay before him, was not altogether devoid of emotion. He felt the separation more than he thought he would.

"Now be a good boy, Bob," counseled his mother.

"I will." "It's your first long trip, and it certainly is a big one," spoke his father. "Prove yourself a man, Bob."

"I'll try, sir."

Bob felt new responsibilities now, and made any number of good resolutions.

"Ahoy, my hearties!" called the bluff, cheerful voice of Captain Spark. "Heave up the anchor, brace around the yards, for we've got a good wind, a free course and a fair sky!"

And with a chorus of good-bys the two started off toward the depot. The trip was begun.

# CHAPTER XI

## THE "EAGLE" SAILS

Bob had often been on railroad journeys, so there was nothing especially interesting about the first part of his trip. But his mind was so taken up with what was to follow that even the familiar scenes as the train sped on out of the village seemed full of delight to him.

"Well, I s'pose you've been pretty steady since I've been gone, haven't you, Bob?" asked the captain, following a rather long pause.

"Well, pretty good, I guess. I only played one joke."

"What was It?"

Bob related the circumstances of the step-ladder, the cook and the hired man.

"Hum," remarked the commander of the *Eagle* reflectively. "So they came down in a heap, eh, and the water splashed all over 'em?"

"Yes," replied Bob, trying not to chuckle at the recollection.

"Hum," remarked the captain again, and he seemed to be having some difficulty with his breathing. Bob wondered if his friend was choking, he was so very red in the face, but he did not know that the mariner was trying hard not to laugh. The thought of the sight of the pair tangled up in the step-ladder was too much for him, though he did not want to encourage Bob in his reckless ways by showing enough interest to laugh.

"By the way," went on the captain suddenly, becoming rather solemn, "I s'pose you've learned the principal parts of the ship by now?"

"By names, yes, sir. But I'm afraid I've got lots yet to learn."

"I should say you had. You know about as much how to sail a ship as I would how to run a steam-engine from seeing a tea-kettle boil."

Captain Spark believed in making boys know their place, and he made up his mind he had a hard subject in Bob. Still, he was determined to reform him if it was possible.

"When do you expect to get into the Southern Pacific?" asked Bob, as he thought of the secret map Captain Obed had given him.

"It all depends on what weather we have. Why?"

"Here's something a friend of mine gave me," said Bob, pulling out the wrinkled piece of parchment. "He says there is treasure buried on an island in the Southern Pacific."

"Treasure? Let me see."

Captain Spark looked critically at the rather faint tracing of lines on the yellow sheet.

"I'm afraid somebody has been playing a joke on you, or on Captain Obed," he remarked, handing the parchment back, after Bob had told him how he became possessed of it.

"A joke?"

Frank V. Webster

"Yes. That's a map, sure enough, but no sailor could ever find the island by those directions."

"Why not?"

"I said he never could. Perhaps I should have said he might by accident. Why, look, Bob. Whoever made this map only marked the location of the Island by degrees; that is the degree of longitude and that of latitude. Every circle is divided into three hundred and sixty degrees, and as the earth is round, It follows that a circle drawn around it would be the same. Each degree therefore means a distance at the equator of about seventy miles. So unless whoever drew this map is positive that the island is exactly at the intersection of the degrees of latitude and longitude which you have given me, it might be seventy miles one way or the other off from the location given here. And seventy miles is a good distance on the water. Besides, the map only states that the location is 'about' right. I guess we'll never find that treasure, Bob. I don't believe it's there."

"Would you think it worth trying for?"

"I don't believe I would. I might have to sail around for a week merely to locate the island, and the chances would be I'd miss it. Then if I did find it, it would be very unlikely that anything would be buried there. I don't take any stock in those Captain Kidd yarns. There's too many of 'em being spun by retired sailors. If Captain Kidd had any money, he took good care of it, you can wager. Besides, I haven't any time to fool around looking for an island. I have to get my cargo to port on time."

Bob was a little disappointed that he could not take part in a search for Captain Obed's treasure, but he reflected that what Captain Spark said was probably right, resides, no one ever believed the stories Captain Obed told. The aged man's mind was not to be depended on.

During the remainder of the journey by rail Captain Spark gave Bob some good advice as to how to conduct himself while aboard the ship. He imparted some useful information concerning navigation, and promised to show Bob more about it after they had sailed.

"I'm anxious to get out on deep water," said the mariner. "I don't like this city life. There are too many risks in it."

In due time they arrived at the seaport town, and, having seen that Bob's baggage would be transported to the dock, Captain Spark led the way to where the *Eagle* was waiting the hoisting of her white sails to catch the ocean breezes.

The ship was a large one, square-rigged, and had three masts, it being of good tonnage. As the voyage was a long one great care had to be taken in loading the cargo, and this had caused a little delay. Not all the freight was aboard yet.

"Well, Mr. Carr, how are things moving?" asked the captain of a tall, thin man who stood near the gangway as he and Bob went up the plank.

"Very well, sir. I think we shall be loaded by to-morrow."

"I hope so. This lying at dock doesn't suit me. By the way, let me introduce a friend of mine. This is Bob Henderson. His mother is a relative of mine, and Bob is taking a voyage for his health. Bob, this is my first mate, Mr. Carr."

"He looks healthy enough," remarked the first mate as he cordially shook hands with Bob.

"Things are not always what they look like," replied the captain with a smile. "Bob found matters rather too lively for him ashore, and his folks think it will quiet him down to go with me."

"I see," replied Mr. Carr in answer to his commander's sly wink. He now understood something of the situation.

"I'll leave you here a while," went on the commander to the boy. "You can look about a bit while I go below and work on my manifest. Mr. Carr will tell you anything you want to know."

But Bob was so interested in watching the sailors at work stowing away the cargo, while others were cleaning various parts of the ship, that he did not ask many questions.

All the rest of that day the loading went on. Bob and the captain went ashore for their meals, as the commander had some business to attend to in the port, but Bob spent that night in his bunk. It was the first time he had ever slept in a ship's berth, and he rather liked the novelty.

The next day the loading was rapidly proceeded with, and by noon all the cargo was stowed away.

Captain Spark was below in his cabin, making out the final papers and waiting for his clearance documents from the harbor master. Mr. Carr and his assistants were busy getting the *Eagle* ready to sail, while Bob stood near the rail, watching with curious eyes everything that was going on.

While he stood there he saw a short, stout, pale-faced man coming up the gangplank. The man carried a valise in each hand, while behind him walked a 'longshoreman with a trunk on his shoulder.

"Now, my man, be very careful of that trunk," urged the short, stout, pale man. "Don't drop it for the world."

"I'm not going to, sir," and the 'longshoreman attempted to touch his hat as a mark of respect.

"Don't do that!" exclaimed the nervous man. "You might drop it, and something would break."

"All right, sir. Very well, sir," and once more the

'longshoreman made as if to touch his hat. It was a habit of his to do this whenever spoken to by those who employed him.

"There you go again!" cried the man in rather whining tones. "Don't do it, I say! There! Keep your hands on the trunk!"

Seeing that this last order was obeyed, the nervous man advanced up the gangplank. He came on deck, set his two valises very carefully down, watched the 'longshoreman place the trunk on end, as if it contained eggs, and then he asked of Bob:

"Is this ship the *Eagle?*"

"Yes, sir."

"Are you sure now? I don't want any mistake made. I don't see the name on it anywhere."

"It is on the bows and under the stern."

Bob rather prided himself on this nautical knowledge.

"Hum! Well, perhaps it may be. You are positive it is the *Eagle?*"

"Yes, sir.  Positive. A distant relative of my mother is the captain."

"Is it Captain Spark?"

"Yes, sir."

"Are you sure? I don't want to be on the wrong ship."

"Yes, sir, I am very sure, I came on board with him. Are you going to sail on the ship?" asked Bob politely.

"I expect to, if this is the right vessel. I wish I was sure. Perhaps you might be mistaken," and he glanced nervously around.

"No, I am positive. There is Captain Spark now," he added as the commander came up a companionway.

"Oh, yes. I shall speak to him."

The nervous man started off. Just then Captain Spark, having received his clearance papers by messenger, gave orders to cast off. The *Eagle* was about to sail.

"All ashore that's going ashore!" called the first mate.

The 'longshoreman started down the gangplank which was about to be hauled in.

"Wait, I must pay you!" called the nervous passenger, turning back toward the man who had brought his trunk aboard.

The 'longshoreman waited.

"Cast off that stern line!" shouted the captain.

"Oh, dear! I wish I was sure this was the *Eagle*!" spoke the nervous passenger.

"It is," Bob assured him, smiling at the man's manner. First he would advance a little way toward the captain, intending to ask him the momentous question; then he would turn toward the 'longshoreman, who was waiting for his money.

"Lively with that gangplank now!" ordered the commander.

"Oh, if I have made a mistake and gotten on the wrong ship it will be terrible," murmured the man.

"Why don't you throw off that stern line?" again shouted the captain.

"What shall I do?" exclaimed the nervous man.

"If you're goin' t' pay me, your honor, you'll have t' hustle," advised the 'longshoreman.

"I will, my man. Never mind touching your hat. Oh, you are not carrying my trunk now; I forgot. Here's a dollar. Never mind the change."

"All ashore that's going ashore!" yelled Mr. Carr again.

Up came the gangplank. The 'longshoreman leaped over the side of the ship and landed on the dock. There was a puffing from the tug that had been engaged to pull the *Eagle* out into the channel.

"Are you sure this is the right ship?" appealed the man to Bob once more.

"Positively yes, sir. Anyhow, it's too late now."

"Too late? How? What do you mean?"

"I mean that we're under way now."

The nervous passenger ran to the side and looked over. True enough, the *Eagle* was some distance from the wharf. The tug was straining on the big hawser. The ship had begun her long voyage around Cape Horn.

Frank V. Webster

# CHAPTER XII

## SOME JOKES ON BOB

Seeing that he was now indeed afloat, and that the ship was some distance from land, the man became more nervous than ever. He paced up and down the deck, looking anxiously at the fast-receding shore.

Suddenly he ran toward the bow of the ship and leaned far over the rail.

"Hey there!" yelled Bob, thinking the man was going to Jump overboard and swim ashore. "What are you doing?"

"I was trying to see the name of the vessel," answered the man, whose face was now red instead of pale, caused by his exertion in bending over the rail.

"You can't see it by leaning over," replied Bob. "It's painted away up by the figurehead."

"I know I can't see it," answered the nervous passenger. "Oh, I wish I was sure."

"I tell you you're on the *Eagle*," declared Bob. "Can't you take my word?"

"When you get as old as I am, and have been through as much trouble, you'll never take anybody's word for anything," was the answer. "I must be sure. I'm off for a long voyage, and I don't want to make a mistake."

"You're not making any mistake if you want to be aboard the *Eagle*. Here comes Captain Spark now. You can ask him."

At that moment the commander, having seen his vessel well under way, came to where Bob and the nervous passenger were standing.

"Is this Mr. Hiram Tarbill?" asked the mariner, holding out his hand.

"Yes, sir. Are you Captain Jeremiah Spark?"

"That's who I am."

"Is this the schooner *Eagle*, bound around Cape Horn?"

"Yes, sir, with a mixed cargo consigned to various firms in Lima, Peru. Would you like to look at my papers?"

"No, I guess it's all right," and Mr. Tarbill seemed much relieved. "You see, my train was late," he went on, "and I came aboard in such a hurry that I was not sure I was on the right ship. I dislike to make mistakes, especially as my health is not very good."

"Yes, you're on the right ship," Captain Spark assured Mr. Tarbill. "Now if you'll come with me I'll show you to your stateroom. But first let me introduce to you a relative of mine," and he presented Bob.

"Yes, I have been talking with him," said Mr. Tarbill. "He assured me I was on the right vessel, but I did not know whether he knew or not."

"Oh, yes, Bob knows that much about the ship. But he's going to learn more soon."

The captain conducted the nervous passenger to the stateroom set apart for him and then came back on deck.

"What do you think of him?" he asked Bob.

"He seems all right, but very nervous."

"That's the trouble. He's too nervous. His doctor recommended him to take a long sea voyage to see if it would cure him. I think it will. I never knew a sailor who was nervous, and it's all because of the salt water. Now, Bob, amuse yourself as best you can until the tug drops us. I have several matters to attend to. After a bit I'll give you some regular duties to perform every day. They will not be hard, but I shall expect you to perform them as well as you are able. While in the main this is a pleasure trip for you, undertaken for a purpose with which you are familiar, I want you to derive some benefit from it. Don't you think that wise?"

"Yes, sir," answered Bob, who had formed several good resolutions regarding his future conduct.

"Very well, then. You can roam about the ship at your pleasure until I am ready for you."

Now a ship is one of the best places in the world for the circulation of news. It is a little village in itself, and what happens in the captain's cabin, though there may be a desire to keep it secret, is soon known in the forecastle, or "fo'kesel," as the sailors pronounce it. Consequently it was not long before it was known that Bob was being sent on the voyage to reform him for certain roguish tricks to which he was addicted. This was known to the majority of the crew before the ship sailed.

Consequently they were not only on their guard against any pranks which the boy might try to perpetrate, but several of the younger men resolved to give Bob a taste of his own medicine.

There was some whispering among members of the crew as they observed Bob strolling about the deck, and one of the men said something to Mr. Carr. The first mate nodded and smiled. A little later, as Bob was watching the men coil up the big hawser which the tug had cast off, the *Eagle* now proceeding along under her own sails, one of the sailors stepped up to him.

"Would you mind doing us a favor?" he asked respectfully.

"Of course not. I'll do anything I can for you," answered Bob, glad to make the closer acquaintance of the men.

"Then would you kindly go to Captain Spark and ask him for a left-handed marlinspike? We need it to splice this hawser with. He keeps it in his cabin because there's only one on board and it's quite a valuable instrument."

The man spoke as gravely as a judge.

"A left-handed marlinspike?" repeated Bob. "I suppose one of the sailors must be left-handed," he thought.

He knew what a marlinspike was from having seen the men use the sharp-pointed irons to pick apart the strands of rope preparatory to splicing, so, anxious to be of service, he hurried to Captain Spark's cabin.

"The men sent me for a left-handed marlinspike," he said, interrupting the commander, who was busy over his accounts.

"A left-handed marlinspike," repeated the commander, at once understanding the joke.

"Yes, sir."

"I'm sorry," was the answer, gravely given, "but I lost it overboard a while ago. You'd better go to Mr. Carr and ask him for the scuttle-butt. That will do as well."

Frank V. Webster

"Yes, sir," replied Bob, who, not suspecting anything, hunted up the first mate and made his request.

"You'll find it right over there," said Mr. Carr, pointing to a big water barrel on deck. It was one from which the sailors drank. "If it's too heavy for you, you'd better get help," said Mr. Carr, trying not to smile. But Bob was aware now that he had been made the butt of a joke, and though he felt a little embarrassed, he had to laugh in spite of himself.

"That's pretty good," he said. "A left-handed marlinspike turns into a scuttle-butt, and that turns into a water barrel. I've got lots to learn yet."

He could hear the sailors laughing at the trick they had played, with the consent of the first mate, and with a grim smile Bob resolved to get even.

# CHAPTER XIII

## BOB TRIES A PRANK

The *Eagle* was sailing along under a spanking breeze, and already the motion of Old Briny was beginning to make itself felt. The vessel rolled to a considerable degree, and as she passed farther and farther out to sea this became more pronounced.

Bob, who had been active in visiting different parts of the ship, watching the sailors at their duties, and picking up bits of information here and there, soon got over his little indignation against those who had played the joke on him. But he soon became conscious of another feeling.

This was a decidedly uneasy one, and for the first time since he had begun to think of the voyage Bob began to fear he was going to be seasick.

"I certainly do feel queer," said our hero to himself as he leaned against the railing amidships. "I wonder what I'd better do? Perhaps I'm moving around too much. I'll keep quiet."

He sat down on a hatch cover and tried to think of other things. The sea was beginning to turn blue—the blue of deep water—and the sun was shining brightly. There was a strong wind and a healthful smell of salt in the air.

Still Bob did not appear to care for any of those things. His

Frank V. Webster

own feelings seemed to increase.

"Sitting still is worse than moving around," he began to think.

Just then Mr. Carr passed the boy.

"What's the matter?" he asked. "You look rather white about the gills, messmate."

"I—I don't feel very well," replied Bob.

"Better go and lie down then. I guess you're in for a spell of seasickness. Mr. Tarbill has already got his."

Bob thought it would be best to follow the advice. He went to his berth, and soon he was a very sick boy. He would have given up all his chances of rounding the Horn—yes, he would even have sacrificed his share in the rather mythical treasure of Captain Obed—if he could only have found some place that was not heaving, pitching and tossing. But the ship rolled on, and the motion seemed to increase rather than diminish.

It was a week before Bob was entirely well. During that time he stayed in his bunk, but Captain Spark saw to it that the boy was well looked after and doctored with such simple remedies as are used in that common form of illness, which attacks nearly all who first venture upon the sea.

At the end of the week Bob found that he could stand up without feeling his head go buzzing around. He ventured out on deck, and the salt breeze brought some color into his pale cheeks.

"You sort of look as if you had been drawn through a knot-hole," remarked Tom Manton, one of the sailors.

"Yes, old Father Neptune has been playing tricks on him, I reckon," added Sam Bender, the second mate.

"I feel as if I had been drawn through two knot-holes, one right after the other," spoke Bob, with an attempt at a smile.

"You'll soon be all right again now," comforted Tom. "Get a little salt horse and sea biscuit down for a foundation, and you can build up on that the finest thing in the way of a meal you ever saw."

For the first time since his illness Bob could think of food without a shudder. He really began to feel hungry. The old sailor proved a good prophet. Bob began to mend steadily, and in a few days he was as active as ever—more so, in fact.

"Now's the time to look for trouble," remarked Captain Spark to his mate one day.

"Trouble? How?"

"Bob is himself again. He'll be up to some tricks or I'm a Dutchman. But we must meet him half way. Give him back some of his own coin. He's on this voyage to be cured, and I'm going to do it If I have to keelhaul him."

"I guess the men will be only too anxious to do their share. They like Bob, but he mustn't play too many pranks on them."

"No. Well, I guess they can look out for themselves."

"I guess so," answered the mate with a smile. Later that day Captain Spark instructed Bob in some simple duties which would be his to perform during the voyage. He was to act in the capacity of cabin boy.

Now that Bob was in his usual spirits he began to feel an inclination to be at some of his pranks. He thought, with a sigh, that he had not played a good joke since the affair of the step-ladder, the cook and the hired man. So he began to look about and consider the possibilities of indulging in some pranks.

But Bob had about made up his mind not to bother the sailors. He was a little afraid of them, as they were big, strong men, and he had a suspicion that they were only waiting for him to begin operations before they would do something on their own account. Bob had an idea they might tie him to a rope, throw him overboard and duck him.

That, he thought, would be pretty harsh treatment.

"I wish Mr. Tarbill would come from his stateroom," Bob mused. "I guess it would be safe to play a little joke on him. I've simply got to have some fun."

Mr. Tarbill had suffered very much from seasickness, though he was now recovered. He came on deck the next day, but he was more nervous than ever.

"Oh, my!" he exclaimed as a big wave struck the *Eagle*, heeling her over considerably. "Are we going down?"

"Oh, I guess not," replied Bob confidently. He and Mr. Tarbill were together on the quarterdeck. The nervous passenger's fears gave Bob an idea.

"I'll give him a real scare," thought the boy. "Maybe it will cure him of being nervous."

My reader can easily understand that Bob had one thought for Mr. Tarbill and two for himself.

The boy considered matters a few minutes, during which time the nervous passenger seemed to grow more and more frightened of the big waves, which had been piled up by quite a heavy blow the previous night.

Presently Bob went to the after-rail and looked intently into the water. Then he uttered an exclamation.

"Oh! Oh!" he cried. "It's coming right after us! Have you a revolver, Mr. Tarbill?"

"A revolver? What for? What is coming after us, my dear young friend?"

"A big whale! He's just under the surface of the water! He's trying to break off the rudder! Quick, give me your revolver!"

"I haven't any! Oh, dear! I'm so nervous! Do you think he will damage the ship, my dear young friend?"

"I'm afraid so! Look out! Hold on! Here he comes!"

Bob pretended to grasp the rail to prevent being tossed overboard by the expected shock. Mr. Tarbill did the same, and with anxious fears waited for what would happen next. Then the ship seemed to give a great shiver as a big wave struck under the port bow.

"He's hit us!" cried Bob, trying not to laugh.

"Quick! Get me a life-preserver!" exclaimed Mr. Tarbill. "A life-preserver! The ship is sinking!"

"What's all the excitement about?" suddenly asked Captain Spark, appearing at the head of the ladder that led to the quarterdeck.

"The ship has been struck by a monster whale!" exclaimed the nervous passenger, "He's rammed us, captain, and I'm going to get a life-preserver! Then I must save my valuables in my cabin!"

He rushed from the deck, while the captain, with a grim look on his face, glanced at Bob, who burst into laughter.

# CHAPTER XIV

## MR. TARBILL GETS A SHOCK

"This is one of your 'jokes,' I suppose," remarked the captain.

"Yes. It was too funny," answered Bob. "He really believed a whale was after us."

"Do you think it was a good thing to do, alarm him so?"

"I—er—well, I thought it might do his nerves good," stammered Bob.

"Hum!" murmured the captain. "I must say, Bob, you have a queer idea of what is good for the nerves. Now I can't allow this. Mr. Tarbill is a guest of mine, and I will not have his comfort interfered with. He is taking a voyage for his health, and I don't want him annoyed."

"I'm sorry," began Bob, always ready to repent, though usually it did not last long.

"Then don't do it again."

"I'll not, sir. I didn't think he'd believe me."

"He knows very little about the ocean. In fact, there are some things you don't know, and, if they wanted to, some of the old sailors could spin you yarns that would make your hair stand up."

"I wish they would then," said Bob. "I like sea stories, captain."

"I guess I'll have to take stronger measures with him," thought the commander as he walked forward.

A few minutes later Mr. Tarbill rushed up on deck. He had a life-preserver strapped about him, and in either hand was a valise, while over his shoulder was some spare clothing he had not had time to pack in the satchels.

"Are the lifeboats ready?" he asked of Mr. Carr, who was the first person he met on deck.

"The lifeboats? What for?"

"Why, the ship has been rammed by a whale and is sinking."

"Who told you so?"

"That boy, Bob Henderson."

"I thought so!" exclaimed the mate. "That's one of his so-called 'jokes.' There's no danger, Mr. Tarbill. That was only a big wave that hit us. You are perfectly safe."

"Are you sure?"

"Quite sure."

"Don't you think I had better see the captain and ask him about it before I take off my life-preserver?"

"Oh, no; there is no need of that. The ship is in no danger," and the mate tried not to smile at the nervous passenger's fears.

"Then if you say so I'll go and take this life-preserver off. It is quite heavy."

"Do so by all means. The young rascal," added the mate under his breath as he thought of Bob. "I'll have to teach him a lesson."

Bob was not a little alarmed at the result of his thoughtless prank. He did not know what the captain might do to punish him, and in the future he resolved to restrain his impulses.

"Maybe he'll send me home by some passing ship," the boy thought, "and I wouldn't like that a bit."

The weather was fine for the next few days. The *Eagle* continued on her way south, the climate getting warmer and warmer as they approached the equator. Bob meanwhile had learned much about the ship and the manner of sailing it. He got the names of the various ropes and sails by heart, and it would have taken a pretty ingenious sailor to have sent him on a foolish errand now after some part of the ship's gear. Captain Spark was encouraged by Bob's behavior, and began to think the voyage was doing the lad good. So it was, but the cure was not complete, as you shall see.

Mr. Tarbill resented Bob's joke, and had not spoken to the boy since the "whale" incident. But Bob did not mind this. There was plenty to keep him occupied, with his duties to perform and sailors' stories to listen to.

When they were out about two weeks there came a day when there was only the lightest breeze, The *Eagle* barely had steerageway over the sea, which was as quiet and still as a small lake. The blue waters sparkled in the bright sun, and as Bob lounged about on deck he felt a lazy contentment which was probably caused by the near approach to the tropical zone.

He looked up at the towering masts, and an idea came to him.

"If I could climb up there," he said, "I could have a fine view. I ought to be able to see a vessel from that height. Guess I'll do it. I never tried it, but it looks easy, and there's not enough motion to pitch me off."

With Bob, usually, to think was to act. Looking around to see that neither the captain nor the mates were in sight to forbid him, he stepped to the rail, mounted Into the shrouds, or ladders, that are formed by the wire ropes supporting the mast, and was soon ascending toward the maintop, the highest point of the largest mast.

It was rather difficult work, but Bob kept on and soon was a great distance above the deck. He looked around him, noted several ships which were not visible from below and then glanced down. He saw Mr. Tarbill come out on deck, and then, more in good spirits than because he wanted, to cause the nervous passenger a scare, Bob gave a great shout. Mr. Tarbill looked up, saw the boy far in the air, clinging to what, at that distance, Seemed but a slender stick, and then he cried:

"Quick! Somebody come quick!"

"What is it?" shouted Mr. Carr, thinking from the tones of Mr. Tarbill's voice some one had fallen overboard.

"That boy! That awful boy!" replied the nervous man.

"What about him? Is he overboard? Which side? I'll throw him a life-preserver!"

"No, he isn't overboard! He's up there! On the mast! Oh! Suppose he falls! My nerves are in such a state! This is an awful shock! What a dreadful boy! I wish he had never come aboard this ship, or else that I hadn't!"

"Come on up!" cried Bob, all unconscious of the excitement he had created. "It's fine up here!"

"Oh! I feel as if I was going to faint!" exclaimed Mr. Tarbill, growing paler than usual.

"Come down, Bob!" ordered Mr. Carr, making a trumpet of his hands. "If it isn't one thing it's another," thought the mate. "I'll be glad when this voyage is over."

# CHAPTER XV

## THE STORM

Bob came down, wondering why he was not allowed to stay at the maintop for a while longer.

"Oh! Oh!" exclaimed Mr. Tarbill when the boy reached the deck. "You've given me such a fright!"

"I didn't mean to," replied Bob honestly enough.

"Oh, but you did! I think I'll have to go to my cabin and take some nerve medicine."

The passenger left the deck, and Mr. Carr said:

"Don't do that again, Bob."

"No, sir; not if you don't want me to."

"It's too dangerous," added the first mate.

Bob was not very sharply reprimanded by Captain Spark for this escapade, as the commander realized that the boy meant no harm. But it was several days before Mr. Tarbill got over the shock.

Urged on by brisk winds the *Eagle* made excellent speed, and several days before he calculated he would reach it Captain

Frank V. Webster

Spark found his vessel "crossing the line"; that is, passing over the imaginary circle which marks the equator. Bob enjoyed his life on board the ship more than ever, now that the tropics were reached. The usual pranks were indulged in by the sailors when Father Neptune came aboard the day the line was crossed, and Bob came in for not a little horse-play. But he did not mind it, and in turn he played several jokes on the sailors and was not rebuked. It was a time of freedom from restraint.

Continuing on south, the *Eagle* passed from the hot region, and once more was in the temperate zone. But now the weather, which had been fine for several weeks, began to show signs of a change.

"We'll soon be in for a troublesome time," said the captain as he sat in the main cabin one night, looking over some charts.

"How?" asked Bob.

"We're approaching the Horn. To navigate the Straits of Magellan is no small matter. There are always more or less storms in that region, and I wish I was well through it."

"Then we're liable to have a hard passage?" "More than likely."

The captain's fears were verified. A few days later, when they were within a hundred miles of the dreaded Straits, it began to blow. There was a steady increase to the wind, and Captain Spark wore an anxious look as he paced the quarterdeck.

Still there seemed to be nothing more than a heavy blow, and Bob was beginning to hope they might get through with less trouble than the commander anticipated. The captain had decided to try the passage of the Straits rather than to actually go around Cape Horn.

But it was not to be. The next day, toward evening, when they were preparing to navigate the difficult passage, there came a veritable hurricane.

Fortunately Captain Spark had in a measure anticipated it, and had taken in sail, bending on some heavy storm canvas which, small as it was, sent the ship ahead at a terrific pace.

As night came on the *Eagle* was seen to be in a mass of swirling, tumbling waves which seemed anxious to overpower the stanch craft.

Mr. Tarbill was in a great fright. He tried to stay in his cabin, but when the ship began to pitch and toss he could not stand it. So donning a life-preserver, he came on deck. Here he was much in the way, for the sailors had to be constantly rushing here and there, making ropes fast and attending to their duties. To add to the discomforts of the situation, it began to rain in torrents.

"Oh, I know we're going to sink!" cried the nervous passenger. "Do you think it will be soon, captain?"

"What soon?" asked the commander, who was too busy to pay much attention to Mr. Tarbill. "Will we sink soon?"

"Sink? We're not going to sink at all if I can help it! This is no worse than lots of storms. You had better go to your cabin and lie down."

"Oh, I wouldn't dare to! The ship might sink while I was there. I know we'll get caught in a whirlpool, or in a waterspout, or some other dreadful thing! This is terrible! Awful! Fearful!"

The wind was increasing, and great waves dashed over the *Eagle's* bow.

"It's bad luck to have such a storm-croaker as that aboard," murmured one of the sailors. "He's a regular Jonah!"

"I wish he'd go below," muttered the captain, and Bob overheard him. "He's frightening every one up here, and we're going to have a hard enough time as it is without a nervous man on deck."

Bob, though he was frightened at the storm, which was constantly growing worse, determined to stick it out. He wanted to see what would happen. But he saw a chance to do a service to the captain, though it would involve playing an innocent trick on Mr. Tarbill.

Accordingly, when there came a little lull in the wind, Bob made his way to where the nervous passenger stood with his back braced against a deckhouse.

"It'll be here pretty soon now," said Bob, shouting to make himself heard above the noise of the storm.

"What will, my dear young friend?" asked Mr. Tarbill, forgetting his former anger at Bob under the stress of the circumstances. "Do you mean to tell us anything else is going to happen?"

"Something surely is, Mr. Tarbill," said Bob, with an air of great earnestness, moving closer to the man, so as to get away from the driving rain, as Mr. Tarbill stood under shelter.

"What is coming? Do tell me. I am so very nervous."

"The Jilla-Jilly wind! We'll be in the midst of it soon. You'd better look out!"

"The Jilla-Jilly wind? For mercy sakes, what's that?"

"It's a kind of a hurricane," said Bob, inventing something on the spur of the moment. "Only, instead of blowing straight ahead or around in a circle it blows up and down. It's liable to snatch you right up to the clouds, or suck you down into the ocean!"

"That is terrible, my dear young friend!"

"Terrible! I should say it was!"

"What had I better do?"

"You'll surely be blown overboard if you stay on deck. That Jilla-Jilly wind is the most terrible wind you ever heard of! We'll soon strike it! There, that sounds like it now! Don't you feel as if you were being lifted up?"

The nervous fears of Mr. Tarbill made him anticipate almost any sensation that was vividly described to him. He was in such a state of mind that he would have believed almost anything he heard.

"Yes! Yes!" he exclaimed. "I feel it coming! Oh, dear! What shall I do?"

"Go below quickly!" yelled Bob, for that was the object he had in mind in inventing the Jilla-Jilly wind for the occasion.

"I will! I'll go at once!" And, holding on to hand-lines which had been stretched about the deck for safety, the nervous passenger made his way to his cabin, while the ship tossed more than ever.

# CHAPTER XVI

## WRECK OF THE SHIP

Though the vessel was in great danger Bob could not help smiling at the success of his prank. When Mr. Tar-bill, with every evidence of terror, had left the deck, Bob crept cautiously forward to peer ahead into the wild waste of waves that threatened to overwhelm the *Eagle*.

"If it isn't a Jilla-Jilly wind, it's almost as bad," thought our hero. If he had known more about the ocean and its terrors he would have been more frightened than he was. If it was not exactly an instance of "where ignorance is bliss, 'tis folly to be wise," it was, in Bob's case, the next thing to it.

"Wow! That was a bad one!" exclaimed the boy, as an extraordinarily large wave made the ship tremble.

At the same instant a frightened shriek rang out through the darkness. It was one full of terror.

"It's got me! It's got me!" yelled the voice. "What in the world is that?" shouted Captain Spark above the din of the storm. "Is some one overboard?"

"Sounds like Mr. Tarbill," replied the mate, putting his lips close to the captain's ear, so as to be heard.

"Maybe something has happened to him," suggested the

commander. "Better look after him, Mr. Carr. We shall do very well for the time being. We've got her before the gale now, and she's scudding along very nicely."

Once the first fury of the storm was past, and it settled down to a steady blow, Captain Spark knew how to handle his vessel. Mr. Carr went below. He found Mr. Tarbill in the main cabin, pacing to and fro and starting nervously at every unexpected lurch of the ship.

"Is it blowing? Is the ship going up or down?" asked the nervous passenger.

"Is what blowing?"

"The Jilla-Jilly wind!"

"The Jilla-Jilly wind?" repeated the mate in wonder, thinking Mr. Tarbill might be out of his head.

"Yes, Bob told me about it. It blows up and down and is liable to take one up Into the clouds or down into the ocean."

"What nonsense! Look here, Mr. Tarbill, that was one of Bob's jokes. I'll scold him for this."

Yet, secretly, the mate was not sorry that Bob's trick had been effective in getting the frightened man off the deck.

"Then there isn't any such wind?"

"Of course not. Don't be frightened."

"Is the ship in any danger?"

"Well, to be honest, I can't say that she is not. There is always danger in a storm such as this is, particularly near Cape Horn. But we're doing our best."

"Oh! I knew something was going to happen!"

"What's going to happen?" asked the mate. "You must not be so nervous."

"Oh! I wish I had never come on this dreadful voyage!"

Mr. Carr wished the same on behalf of the nervous man, but he said nothing. The mate soon went back on deck, where he found plenty to do, as one of the storm sails had blown off the bolt ropes and another canvas had to be bent on. Captain Spark had sent Bob below, as it was risky for any one but an experienced sailor to move about the constantly sloping deck.

That night was one of terror. First the storm seemed to abate, and then it began again with redoubled violence. Once the *Eagle* was almost on her beam ends, but skilful handling brought her once more up into the teeth of the wind and she rode the waves lightly, like the gallant craft she was.

The nervousness of Mr. Tarbill increased. He would not stay alone in his cabin, and finally begged for Bob to keep him company. Bob was a little diffident about going in, after the trick he had played, but the nervous passenger seemed to forget all about that. The two sat up and talked instead of going to their berths, for sleep was out of the question amid the howling of the gale.

It was nearly morning when Captain Spark, wearing an anxious look, came into the cabin.

"Has the ship foundered? Has it sprung a leak?" asked Mr. Tarbill, for he saw that something was troubling the commander.

"No, we are safe yet," replied Mr. Spark gravely. "But I think you had better put on life-preservers."

"Why?" asked Bob, beginning to feel a nameless fear.

"We are approaching a dangerous reef. If this wind holds we can barely wear off enough to pass it. If we strike it that will be the last of the *Eagle*. We are going to do our best to wear the ship off, but we may not succeed. It is best to be prepared."

At this ominous warning Mr. Tarbill seemed to collapse. However, with Bob's help he donned one of the cork jackets, and the boy did likewise. Captain Spark would not allow them on deck, but promised to give them timely warning if the ship struck.

Then came an hour of anxious waiting. Outside there sounded the dash of rain, the screaming of the wind, and the rush of sailors about the deck as they hastened to obey the captain's commands.

Then, very gradually, there seemed to come a slack in the storm. The ship rode more easily, and Bob began to take heart. A little later Mr. Carr came down into the cabin. He breathed a sigh of relief as he said:

"We're all right. We've passed the reef and we have nothing more to fear for the present. The gale is going down."

"That's the best news I've heard in a year!" exclaimed Mr. Tarbill. "Never again will I take a sea voyage for my health. I've lost seven pounds to-night, I know I have."

Mr. Carr's words were soon verified. When morning broke the wind and rain had ceased, though there was still a heavy sea on, which made the *Eagle* toss and pitch in a dangerous way.

Bob managed to get out on deck, however, and, through the clear atmosphere that followed the storm, he saw the dim outlines of Terra del Fuego—"The Land of Fire"—as part of the end of the South American continent is called.

They finished the passage of the Straits of Magellan without further incident. After that it seemed as if their troubles would be at an end. The sea went down, and, as they made the turn around the South American coast and once more began to approach the equator, the *Eagle* skimmed along like the bird whose name it bore.

"If this weather and the fair breezes keep up," said Captain Spark one day, "we'll arrive ahead of time."

"I guess you didn't think so during the storm, did you?" inquired Bob.

"No indeed! It seemed as if it was going to be touch and go with us one spell. But how do you like your trip—so far?"

"Very much."

"I'm glad of it. I promised your mother it would do you good, and I think it will."

Captain Spark was secretly delighted with the success of his experiment. He thought Bob had given up all his tricks, but that same day showed how much mistaken he was. The boy, seeing a chance to have some sport with one of the sailors—a German—sewed up the sleeves of the man's Jersey. When the man tumbled out of his bunk, in a hurry to take his watch on deck, he could not understand the reason why he could not put on his garment.

"Vot's der madder?" he exclaimed, struggling with the sleeves. "Der vitches haf been at vork! I am bevitched!"

"More like that onery critter of a boy done it," suggested his messmate, a practical Yankee.

"So? I plays a joke on him, alretty yet. Vatch."

And the German was as good as his word. The next afternoon Bob suddenly felt himself being pitched over the rail toward the sea. He yelled and made a grab for the mizzen shroud near which he was standing, but he suddenly found himself brought up with a round turn, for the German had caught the boy's feet in a bight of cable, so that he would not go overboard.

"So!" he exclaimed. "You sews up my sleeves, eh? I t'inks you don't do so no more! Eh?"

"More tricks!" exclaimed the captain, when matters had been explained to him, "I wonder if he'll ever be cured?"

But Bob's cure was nearer at hand than either he or the captain expected.

The fine weather continued for a week, during which time the *Eagle* made good progress. Then came several days of dead calm, when they were near the Tropic of Capricorn, and they suffered much from the heat of the sun.

"I don't like this," remarked Captain Spark one day, as he looked up at the brassy sky.

"Why not?" asked Bob, with the familiarity of a relative.

"I think this means a storm, and we're in a poor location for a bad blow. I don't like it."

As the day wore on it became evident that the captain's prophecy was about to be verified. The wind sprang up suddenly, almost before sail could be shortened, and the *Eagle* heeled over until if seemed as if she would not right. That was the beginning of a storm that was worse than the other.

Scudding along under mere rags of canvas, the ship headed right into the swirl of waters agitated by the wind. As night settled down the captain prepared for the worst. It was evident that he feared something, and every man was on the alert.

The wind increased, but there was no rain. On and on rushed the ship, all through the night. The captain seemed to grow more anxious and would not leave his place at the wheel.

Suddenly, just as the darkness was giving place to the gray light of morning, the *Eagle* hit something. A shiver seemed to run through the whole length of the ship.

"Breakers ahead!" yelled the lookout. "Breakers all around us!"

"I feared as much!" cried the captain. "We've struck on a reef!"

The *Eagle* seemed to back off, probably the recoil from the blow. The wind swirled around, and then, once more, the good ship was driven on the rocks.

Once more she crashed upon the low-lying barrier, and this time an ominous splintering sound followed. There was a terrific crash, and the foremast went by the board. At the same time there was a pounding beneath the bows of the vessel.

"There's a big hole stove in the bows, sir!" cried a sailor, running to Captain Spark. "The water's coming in fast!"

"I'm afraid we're foundering!" added Mr. Carr.

"Stand by to lower the lifeboats!" yelled the captain. "Every man to his place!"

With a great crash the mizzen mast went over the side, crushing one of the lifeboats that hung on davits there.

"What has happened?" yelled Mr. Tarbill, rushing up on deck.

"The *Eagle* is wrecked," replied the captain, speaking calmly, though only a sailor could know what anguish the words cost him.

# CHAPTER XVII

## ADRIFT IN SMALL BOATS

The scene was now one of wild excitement. The sailors were working like Trojans to launch the boats, as it could not be told when the *Eagle* would founder. Already she was settling in the water.

For once Mr. Tarbill seemed too stunned to know what to do. Bob made up his mind to save a few of his own possessions if he could, and he hurried to his berth.

"Put on a life-preserver, Bob," called the captain to him. The boy thought of the time when this order had been given before, but not needed. Now there was real cause for it.

"Oh, Bob! Help me!" pleaded Mr. Tarbill, who was trembling with terror.

"I will. If there's anything valuable in your cabin, you'd better get it out."

"Everything I have is valuable."

"Well, you can't take it all. The boat won't hold it."

"Have we got to go in small boats out on this dreadful ocean?"

"It's the only way to save our lives."

Mr. Tarbill selected some of his possessions, as did Bob, and then the only two passengers on the ship, having donned the cork jackets, went on deck again.

The sailors were busy putting provisions and water into the small boats, of which, fortunately, there were enough to hold all, even with the loss of the one the mast had smashed.

"Is there no way of saving the ship?" asked Bob of the captain as he stood, calm, yet stern, on the quarter-deck.

"No. Her bows are stove in and the foremast has pounded a big hole in her quarter. The *Eagle* is doomed. There must be an uncharted reef about here, or else we were blown off our course."

"Boats are all ready, sir," reported a sailor, running up.

"Very well, tell the men to get in. Mr. Carr will be in command of one boat, Mr. Bender the other, and I will go in my gig. Bob, you and Mr. Tarbill will go with me. Pull well away from the wreck, men, and lay to until we are all together. Then we'll try to get our bearings."

It was getting lighter now, but the storm showed no signs of abating. The *Eagle* was fairly impaled on a sharp point of the sunken reef and was immovable, but the waves were dashing high over the bows.

Suddenly the ship gave a shudder and seemed as if about to tear herself loose, ready to sink beneath the billows.

"Lively, men!" exclaimed the captain. "She'll not last much longer!"

The orders were given to lower the boats. Bob went forward to watch the work, holding on by stray cables that dangled from the wrecked masts.

As the boat of which Mr. Bender was to take charge was being lowered, one of the ropes in the davit pulley, that at the bow, fouled, and, as the sailors at the other davit were letting their line run free, the boat tilted. There was imminent risk of the oars, sail, and mast, besides the supplies, being spilled out. Bob saw the danger and sprang forward with a shout, intending to lend a hand.

As he did so a big piece of one of the yards of the broken mizzen mast which had been hanging by splinters was whipped loose by a gust of wind and fell almost at his feet, missing him by a small margin. Had it struck him squarely it would have killed him.

Bob only hesitated an instant, though the narrow escape gave him a faint feeling in his stomach. Then, before he could make the sailors understand what the trouble was, he grabbed the rope that was running free and, taking a turn about a cleat, prevented the further lowering of the boat.

"Good!" shouted Second-Mate Bender, who had seen what had taken place. "You saved the boat, Bob. In another second all the stuff would have been afloat. Lively now, men. Straighten out that line and lower away. She's settling fast."

In the meanwhile Mr. Carr had succeeded in lowering his boat, and he and his men were in it. The crew of the captain's gig were busy with that craft, and it was all ready to lower.

"Get in, Bob," said the commander of the *Eagle*. "And you too, Mr. Tarbill."

"Aren't you coming?" asked Bob.

"I'm the last one in," was the sad answer, and then the boy understood that the captain is always the last to leave a sinking ship.

"Shall we get in before you lower it?" asked Bob of the sailors who stood at the davit ropes.

"Yes. We can lower it with you two in. The captain and we can slide down the ropes. We're used to it, but it's ticklish business for land-lubbers." And the man grinned even in that time of terror.

Captain Spark had gone to his cabin for his log book, the ship's papers, and his nautical instruments. As he came out the red sun showed for an instant above the horizon.

"If we had seen that a few hours sooner we wouldn't be here now," remarked the commander sadly. "But it's too late now."

The other boats had pulled away from the wreck. Bob and Mr. Tarbill got into the gig and were lowered to the surface of the heaving ocean.

"Take an oar and fend her away from the ship's side a bit," the captain advised Bob. "Else a wave may smash the gig."

Bob did so. Mr. Tarbill was shivering too much with fear to be of any help. A few seconds later the two sailors who had lowered the boat at the captain's orders leaped into the gig as a wave lifted it close to the *Eagle's* rail. Then the commander, carrying a few of his possessions and with a last look around his beloved ship, made the same jump and was in his gig.

"Pull away," he commanded sorrowfully, and the sailors rowed out from the foundered ship.

When they were a little way off they rested on their oars. All around them was a waste of heaving waters. The two other boats came up, and the occupants looked at the *Eagle* settling lower and lower as the water filled her. The wrecked ship, now sunk almost to her deck level, seemed, save for the three boats, to be the only object in sight on the bosom of the tumultuous ocean.

"Well, men, give way!" at length called the captain, with a sigh. "We may be sighted by some vessel, or we may land on an island. There are several islands hereabouts, if we are not too far away from them."

Then, bending to the oars, the sailors sent the boats away from the wreck. Bob and his friends were afloat on the big ocean in small boats that, at any moment, might be swamped by a mighty wave, for the wind was still blowing hard, though the sun shone brightly in the eastern sky.

Frank V. Webster

# CHAPTER XVIII

## BOB ON AN ISLAND

"Keep together, men!" called the captain, as they pulled away. "We don't want to lose one another."

"Which way shall we pull, sir?" asked the first mate.

"I'll tell you presently. I'll look at my charts and see if I can't locate an island somewhere here-abouts. Keep up your courage. Luckily this didn't happen down in the Straits. At least we have warm weather here."

For the first time Bob noticed that it was very warm. It had been so, of course, for several days preceding the wreck, but the thought that they were in a tropical climate had been forgotten in the excitement of the foundering of the ship. Now it was a thing for which to be thankful.

"Oh! Isn't this the most terrible thing that could occur!" exclaimed Mr. Tarbill, from a seat where he was huddled up. "It is awful!"

"It's not half so awful as if we were drowned and in Davy Jones's locker," remarked the captain. "I've lost my ship and the cargo, but, fortunately, both were insured. We are lucky to have had time to get off in the boats, well provisioned as they are. As soon as this wind goes down a bit we'll hoist the small sails and head for the nearest land."

The captain was soon busy over his charts. He made some calculations and announced his belief that there was a group of islands about a hundred miles off. He could not be sure, for while they showed on the chart, he could not exactly determine the position of the ship when she struck, as no observation had been taken since the previous noon, and the rate of sailing under the force of the gale was mere guesswork.

So the men rowed on. The *Eagle* was now a mere blot on the surface of the ocean—a speck of blackness amid a swirl of foam, caused by the waves breaking over the ship and the reef. The wind continued too high to risk raising the sail with which each boat was provided, and it was slow progress with the oars.

The day was one of terror, for many times waves would break over the small craft, forcing the men to bail for their lives. Only cold provisions could be eaten, but in spite of this the little band of shipwrecked men maintained a cheerful demeanor. As for Bob he did not deny that he was frightened. He thought with sorrow of his father and mother and wondered if he would ever see them again. He and the others had removed their life-preservers, as they did not need them in the gig.

"That was a plucky thing you did, saving that boat from going down stern first," complimented the captain, a little later that day when they were talking over the events of the wreck. "You showed good judgment, Bob."

"Oh, I guess anybody would have done the same."

"No, they wouldn't. You deserve great credit. Bravery in the face of danger is bravery indeed. Your father and mother can be proud of you."

There came to Bob's mind a memory of certain times when these words of the captain would not have been true. He resolved, if his life was spared, to be a more manly boy in the future—to live up to the captain's new estimate of him.

Wearily the men labored at the oars. It was hard work to keep the boats' heads to the waves, which, to those in the small craft, looked like great green mountains of water. Now the boats would be down in a vast hollow, with towering walls on either side. Then the stanch craft would be lifted up and, poising on the crests, would slide down a watery hill with a sickening feeling, present at least in the hearts of Bob and Mr. Tarbill, that they were going straight for the bottom. The nervous passenger sat huddled up in a heap, scarcely speaking.

The wind seemed to increase as night drew on. The motion of the captain's gig was such that he could not take an observation, and, when the blackness settled down, they had no idea where they were, nor in which direction the nearest land lay.

"I'm afraid we'll be separated in the darkness," said the captain, "but there is no help for it."

The day of terror was succeeded by a night of peril. The sea and wind seemed combining to wreck the small boats. The one commanded by Mr. Carr managed to remain within hailing distance of the captain's gig, but the other seemed to have disappeared. A feeling of gloom settled down over the castaways.

It must have been about the middle of the night that Bob, working his way aft to get a drink of water from one of the casks, stumbled over part of the sail that was folded in the bottom of the gig. He put out his hands, instinctively, to save himself, but, as there was nothing to cling to, he only grasped the air.

Then, with a cry of terror which he could not suppress, he plunged overboard and was soon struggling in the water.

He went down, but, being a good swimmer, he at once began to strike out, and as he got his head above the surface and shook the water from his ears, he heard one of the sailors cry:

"Bob's overboard!"

"Bob! Bob! Where are you?" shouted the captain. "Here's a life-preserver!"

The boy heard a splash in the water near him and struck out for it.

"Back water!" he heard the captain cry.

"Aye, aye, sir!" replied the sailors heartily.

At the same time the captain shouted to Mr. Carr's boat word of what had happened. Bob was weighted down by his wet clothes and he felt he could not long keep up, but he was swimming strongly, hoping every moment one of the boats would pick him up.

"Here I am!" he shouted, but his voice did not carry far above the wind. He began to have a hopeless feeling, as if he was doomed to drown there all alone on the vast ocean. A nameless terror seized him. Then, to his joy, his fingers touched something. It was the floating cork life-preserver, and he knew he could keep himself up with it for a long time.

Once more he shouted, but there came no answering hail.

"Have they rowed away and left me?" thought the boy.

He held this idea but for an instant. Then he guessed the truth of what had happened. The boats had been swept on by wind and wave, and, in the darkness, it was impossible to see so small an object as the boy's head in the water.

The sailors in the two boats rowed about, frantically urged on by Captain Spark.

"His mother will never forgive me!" he whispered to himself. "I'd rather have lost a dozen ships than have Bob drown!"

But, though they rowed about the spot where he had disappeared, neither the captain nor Mr. Carr nor any of the sailors could find a trace of the boy.

"We'll stand by until morning," decided the commander, and they began their weary vigil.

Meanwhile Bob was swimming right away from the boats, for he could not get the right direction in the darkness. He managed to fasten the life-preserver to him, and with the buoyancy of the cork to aid him he swam easily, though he did not make very fast progress.

After the first shock of terror was over Bob became calm. He had a momentary fear of sharks, but he resolved not to think about these monsters or the sea, as it sent a cold chill over him and he found he could not swim so well.

"I'll just paddle on until morning," he decided, "and by that time maybe the men In the boats will pick me up."

So, through the remainder of the night, he swam leisurely. In spite of the storm it was very warm and the water felt pleasant. If he had only had an idea of where he was, Bob would not have minded his position so very much.

It was just getting light when, happening to let his legs down for an instant to rest them, he felt his feet touch something. At first he had an unreasoning terror that it might be a big fish—a whale or a shark—that had come up under him. Then he felt whatever it was under his feet to be firm and hard. A dim shape loomed up before him.

"It's land!" exclaimed Bob. "I've struck land! It must be one of those islands the captain told about and that is the sandy beach my feet arc touching."

He swam on a little further, and again let down his feet. To his delight he could stand upright, the water coming to his chest.

Then, as it grew lighter, he could make out a low, sandy shore lying stretched out before him.

"Land! Land!" exclaimed the boy. "I'm on land! But where are the others?"

Frank V. Webster

# CHAPTER XIX

## FINDING MR. TARBILL

Bob hurried forward as fast as he could through the water, no longer swimming, but wading. Soon he reached the beach and saw, beyond it, that the land was covered with green grass, while trees, which he easily recognized as the kind found in warm countries, grew to a great height.

"I'm on a tropical island," thought the castaway. "Just like Robinson Crusoe, only I haven't any of the things he had and the wreck of the *Eagle* isn't near enough for me to get anything from the ship. Still I ought to be thankful I'm not drowned or eaten by a shark."

Bob was tired after his long swim and stretched out under the trees on the grass to rest. It was already beginning to get much warmer, though the sun was only just peeping up, seemingly from beneath the ocean.

"Wonder if I'm going to find anything to eat here," the boy thought. "Doesn't look as if any one lived here. I'll have to take a look around. It's going to be very lonesome here. I wonder if any ships ever pass this place?"

There were so many questions that needed answering he did not know where to stop asking them of himself. But he decided the first and best thing to do would be to get off his wet clothes. Not that he was afraid of taking cold, but he knew he would be more comfortable in dry garments.

So, taking everything out of his pockets, which was no small operation by the way, as Bob was a typical boy, he stripped himself of his heavier garments and hung them on tree limbs to dry.

"Now if I could find something to eat I'd be right in it—at least for a while," thought the castaway as he walked around on the warm grass. "And I need a drink, for I swallowed a lot of salt water and I'm as dry as a powder horn." He looked out on the ocean, but not a trace of a boat was visible.

Bob walked some distance from where he had landed, keeping a sharp lookout for a spring of water. Ail the while he was getting more and more thirsty, and he began to think he would have to dig a little well near shore with clam shells, as he had read of shipwrecked sailors doing. But, fortunately, he was not forced to this. As he penetrated a little way into the wood, he heard the gurgle of water.

"That sounds good," he remarked.

Stepping cautiously, because of his bare feet, he went on a little farther and presently saw a small waterfall, caused by a stream tumbling over a little ledge of rocks and splashing into a pool below.

"That looks better than it sounds," thought Bob. And a moment later he was drinking his fill. "Seems as if there might be fish in there," he went on, glancing at the pool. "Guess I'll try it."

Bob was fond of hunting and fishing and knew considerable about wood-lore. Searching under the stones he soon found some worms, and, tossing one into the middle of the pool, he saw a hungry fish rise to it.

"Now if I had a pole, hook, and line I'd soon have a breakfast," he went on to himself. "I have the line, all right, and I ought to have a hook in one of my pockets. I generally do. As for a pole I can easily cut one."

Bob hurried back to where he had piled the things he took from his pockets. It did not take him long to discover that he had a stout cord that would answer for a line, while he also had several hooks. With his knife he cut a pole, and baiting the hook with a worm, he cast in.

Probably no one, unless it might have been some unfortunate castaway in years gone by, had ever angled in that pool. The fish at once rose to the bait, and soon Bob had several beauties on the grass beside him.

"Now to cook them," he said to himself. "Lucky I bought a water-proof match box before I started on this voyage. I can now make a fire."

Bob went back to the place he called "home"—where he had first landed—and looked in the water-tight match box which he always had carried since he had come aboard the *Eagle*. To his delight the little fire-sticks were not harmed by his bath. He only wished he had more of them.

Finding his clothes were now nearly dry, he put part of them on and proceeded to kindle a fire. Then he cleaned the fish and set them to broil by the simple process of hanging them in front of the fire on a pointed stick, one end of which was thrust into the ground.

"That smells good!" exclaimed Bob, as the fish began to brown. "But, I almost forgot. There's plenty of fruit to be had." For he had noticed several trees well laden as he passed through the woods. "I'll not starve here as long as I have fruit and fish."

He gathered some things that looked a cross between an orange and a tangerine and ate several, finding them delicious.

By the time the fish were well done Bob, preparing to eat his odd breakfast, was suddenly startled by a groan. It seemed to come from behind a pile of rocks off to the left.

"I wonder what that was?" thought Bob. "An animal or a human being? I wonder if there are any South Sea natives on this island?"

He put down his fish on some big green leaves he had plucked for plates and went toward the rocks. As he approached, the groans became louder. Peering cautiously over the stones, Bob saw the figure of a man lying on the sand, as if he had managed to crawl out of the water.

For an instant the boy could scarcely believe his eyesight. Then, with a cry, he rushed forward.

"It's Mr. Tarbill!" he exclaimed. "He, too, must have fallen overboard and been washed ashore. But he seems to be hurt."

The man's eyes were closed and he was scarcely breathing.

"He's dying!" thought Bob, his heart beating hard.

Then, thinking perhaps the man might be partly drowned, the young castaway began to put into operation as much of the directions as he remembered for restoring partially drowned persons to life. He had not worked long before he saw Mr. Tarbill's eyes open. Then the nervous passenger began to breathe better.

"Where—where am I?" he asked faintly.

"You're safe," replied Bob. "On an island with me. But where is the captain—and the others?"

"Boat foundered. Wave washed over it—soon after you fell overboard. No chance to get life-preservers. It was every one for himself."

"Are they drowned?"

"I don't know! Oh, it is terrible! I swam as long as I could, then I seemed to be sinking."

"You're all right now," said Bob cheerfully. "You're just in time to have some breakfast."

He helped Mr. Tarbill to his feet. The nervous man seemed to recover rapidly, and when, at Bob's suggestion, he had taken off most of his wet clothes and was drying out near the fire, his face took on a more cheerful look.

"Those fish smell fine," he said. "I'm very fond of fish. Are you sure those are not poisonous?"

"I'm not sure," replied Bob, "and I'm too hungry to care much. They're a sort of big sun-fish, such as I used to catch at home. The meat looks nice and white. Better have some. I'll warm them again."

He put them once more on the pointed sticks near the fire, and when they were sizzling he laid them on the green leaves. Then, with sticks for knives and forks, the two castaways made a fairly good meal.

"I thought I never would see land again," said the nervous man, as he began to dress in his dry clothes after the breakfast. "This has been a terrible experience for me."

"I guess it has," admitted Bob. "And for all of us. I wish I knew what has happened to the captain and the others."

"Our boat was swamped by a big wave," said Mr. Tarbill, "and suddenly we were all thrown into the water. That is the last I remember. Perhaps the captain and some of the crew may have swum ashore on another part of this island."

"I hope so. We'll search for them. I guess we're in for a

long stay."

"Have we got to remain here?" demanded Mr. Tarbill.

"I don't see what else there is to do," replied Bob. "We haven't any boat, we can't walk on the water, and we'll have to stay until a ship comes and takes us off."

"Oh, dear!" exclaimed the nervous man. "I wish I had stayed at home!"

Bob thought he might at least be thankful that his life was spared and that he was not where he would starve, but the lad concluded it would be wise to say nothing.

"If you like we'll take a walk around the island, see how large it is and if there's a place where we can make a sort of shelter," proposed Bob.

"I guess that will be the best thing to do. I leave it all to you. My nerves are in such shape that I can do nothing."

Bob felt not a little proud of the responsibility thus thrust upon him. He resolved to act wisely and cautiously, for there was no telling how long they would have to live on the island.

With the boy in the lead the two started off. The sun was now hot and strong, and they found it advisable to keep in the shade of the woods as much as possible.

Bob saw a big turtle crawling down the beach toward the water, and, knowing the flesh was good for food, he ran forward to catch it. He was too late, however, and when he turned, with a feeling of disappointment, to catch up with Mr. Tarbill, who had continued on, Bob was surprised to hear the man utter an exclamation. He had come to a halt near a pile of rocks and was looking over the tops.

"What's the matter?" asked the boy.

"There are two men down there on the beach! Perhaps they are cannibals! We had better go back!"

"Let me take a look," proposed Bob.

Cautiously he went forward, gave one glance at the figures to which Mr. Tarbill pointed, and then he uttered a cry.

"Hurrah!" he shouted. "They are Captain Spark and Tim Flynn, one of the sailors! They've managed to get to shore! Ahoy, captain! Ahoy! Here we are!" and he ran down the beach toward them.

# CHAPTER XX

## MAKING THE BEST OF IT

Captain Spark and the sailor turned at the sound of Bob's voice. The captain gave a joyful cry and started forward. But Tim Flynn, the sailor, with a yell of fear, ran off down the beach in a different direction.

"Here! Come back!" cried the captain, pausing. "What's the matter with you, Tim?"

"Sure I don't want to meet no ghost!" exclaimed the man.

"Ghost? What do you mean?"

"Him," replied Tim, pointing a shaking finger at Bob. "Didn't we see him drown, an' now ain't he here ahead of us to haunt us? Let me go, cap'n."

He was about to run off again, but Bob, who began to understand the superstitious rears of the man, called out:

"It's me, Tim! I'm alive, all right!"

The sailor paused, turned, and, after a long and rather doubting look at the boy, came slowly bade.

"Well, maybe it's all right," he said, "but it's mighty queer. How'd ye git here?"

"Swam until I struck land. But how did you get here, captain?" and Bob clasped his relative warmly by the hand.

"Our boat must have been close to the island when it capsized," replied the former commander of the *Eagle*. "A big wave did the business for us, and then it was every man for himself. Poor Tarbill, he's lost, and so is Pete Bascom. We'll never see either of 'em again. And I'm afraid the rest of the crew are gone, too. No boat could live long in that sea."

"Mr. Tarbill is alive," said Bob.

"How do you know?"

"He's right behind those rocks. He didn't come on because he feared you were cannibals. I'll call him."

Bob set up a shout, and in a few seconds the nervous passenger came cautiously over the top of a pile of stones. When he saw Captain Spark he was reassured and advanced boldly. There was a general shaking of hands, and then the captain remarked:

"Well, now we're here we'll have to sec what we can find in the way of food and shelter. I don't believe this island is inhabited. I didn't know we were so near one. It isn't down on the charts."

"There is plenty of fish and fruit," said Bob, telling how he had used his hook and line to advantage.

"Good!" exclaimed the captain. "I could eat a fish raw, I believe, and my mouth is dry for need of some fresh water."

"Then come on to my camp," said Bob, proudly leading the way.

The captain could not but note the change in the boy. He had a confident air about him now, as if he could take charge of matters. The experience of the shipwreck, terrible as it had been, had taught Bob some needed lessons. But he had yet more to learn.

While Captain Spark and Tim Flynn were wringing the water out of their heavier garments Bob replenished the fire and soon had some fish broiling, for he had caught more than he needed. It did not take long to finish the simple meal, and then the captain spoke.

"We'd better take a survey of the island," he said, "to see what sort of a place we've landed on. If there are any natives here we want to know it. We also want to know what we can expect in the way of things to eat and if there are animals on it. I don't believe there are, however, as the place is too small."

"Let's start right away," proposed Bob. "Perhaps we can find some driftwood, or something to make a hut of, though it's warm enough to sleep out of doors without shelter."

"But not exactly safe in tropical countries," objected the captain. "I hope we can construct some kind of a house. If we can't we'll have to make the best of it, though, for we haven't any tools to work with, except knives."

They started to make a circuit of the island. It was not very large, being about two miles across. The center was thickly wooded with tropical growth, and the captain was glad to note that there were several varieties of good fruit, including a number of cocoanut trees.

"If worst comes to worst we can make a hut of cocoanut leaves," he said. "The natives often do that."

"Oh, dear! I hope there are no cannibals here," said Mr. Tarbill at the mention of the word natives. "Suppose they should eat us up?"

"They'd have to fight first," observed the captain grimly. "I'll not be eaten without a struggle."

"But I never fought a cannibal in my life," objected the nervous castaway. "I shouldn't know how to go about it."

"No more would I, but I'd soon learn. But don't think about such things, Mr. Tarbill."

"I can't help it. I wonder how long it will be before we are rescued?"

"That is a grave question," said the captain slowly. "I fear this island is too far out of the regular course of ships to hope that we will be picked up soon. We must make some kind of a distress signal and hoist it where it will be seen. We'll do that as soon as we have completed the circuit of the island."

It was long past noon, to judge by the position of the sun, when they had circled the island and again reached the place where Bob had built the fire. They had seen no signs of natives, nor any of animals, though there might be small beasts.

"Well, we know what to expect now," said the Captain, as they sat down under the trees to talk matters over. "We'll have to depend for a living on fish, turtles, and fruit. We have no natives to fear, and our situation is not so bad as it might be. Now we had better set about matters in a shipshape and orderly fashion. In the first place we will name our island. There's nothing like having an address where your friends can write to you," he added, with grim humor.

"Let's call it 'Lonely Land,'" suggested Bob.

"I have a better name," said the commander. "It is the custom to call islands and mountains after the person who discovers them. I propose that we name this 'Bob's Island,' for he discovered it first."

"Aye, aye, sir!" cried Tim Flynn heartily.

Bob blushed and was about to protest, but, to his surprise, Mr. Tarbill joined in and favored the proposition.

"That's settled, then," spoke the captain. "Now you needn't say anything, Bob, we're three to one, and we're going to have our way. So far so good. The next thing is to rig up our distress signal. I'll leave that to Flynn. Tim, climb the highest tree you can find and run up a signal."

"Aye, aye, sir," replied the sailor, saluting and starting off.

"Now then, we'd better catch some more fish for dinner," the captain continued. "I'll leave that to you, Bob, and I'll build another fire, for this one is out. Mr. Tarbill can go and see if he can't catch a couple of turtles."

"Turtles! I never caught a turtle in my life!" exclaimed the nervous man. "I'd be afraid to!"

"Not the least danger," the captain assured him. "All you have to do is to get between them and the water as they're on the beach sunning themselves and turn them on their backs. They'll stay there until I can come and get them. It's time you learned to catch turtles."

"Oh, dear!" sighed Mr. Tarbill. "I wish I was safe home!"

But the captain paid no attention to his protest.

"It'll do him good," he murmured, as the nervous one walked dejectedly off. "He'll not have any nerves left when we get through with him."

Bob had good luck with his hook and line and soon returned with a dozen fine fish. In the meanwhile the captain had built a big fire and had a bed of red coals ready to broil the fish over, for he knew just how to do it.

When the dinner was in process of cooking Tim returned.

"Did you hoist the signal?" asked the captain.

"Aye, aye, sir."

"What did you use for a flag?"

"My shirt, sir."

"Your shirt?"

"Aye, aye, sir. You see I had two on, an outer shirt and an inner shirt. I didn't need the outer shirt as it's so hot here, so I hoisted that on top of a tall tree. It's flying in the breeze now, sir. You can see it from here."

He led the way down to the edge of the water and pointed inland. Sure enough, flying from a tall cocoanut tree was a white shirt. It could be seen for a long distance.

"That's a fine idea," complimented the captain. "I forgot when I sent you off that you hadn't any signal flag. But here comes Mr. Tarbill. I wonder if he turned any turtles? Any luck?" he called as the nervous man approached.

"No, sir. The turtles all ran when they heard me coming. Some of them left a lot of eggs behind."

"Did you bring any?"

"No. I didn't think they were good."

"Good? Of course they're good! We'll gather some later. But come on. It's long past dinner time and I guess we're all hungry."

Every one proved it by the manner in which he ate. The meal was a primitive one, with sticks for forks, though they all had pocket-knives, which answered very well to cut the fish. For plates Captain Spark substituted large clam shells, in place of the leaves Bob had used.

"Now I think we had better rig up some kind of a hut for shelter against the night dews," proposed the captain, when they were done eating. "Gather all the cocoanut leaves you can and I'll make a sort of framework."

Bob started up, ready to go off into the forest after leaves, with the sailor and Mr. Tarbill. As he gazed out to sea, where the big waves were still rolling, he saw something that caused him to utter a cry of astonishment.

"What is it?" asked Captain Spark, hurrying to Bob's side.

"There," replied the boy, pointing to some dark object that was rising and falling on the swell.

"It's a boat! A boat capsized!" exclaimed Captain Spark. "We must secure it. It's one from the *Eagle*. Probably the one we were in."

"Shall I swim out to it?" asked Bob. "Perhaps I can tow it in."

"No, the current is setting toward the beach. It will drift in presently."

# CHAPTER XXI

## MORE ARRIVALS

All interest in building a hut was temporarily forgotten as the four castaways watched the slow approach of the boat. As it came nearer it was seen to be the captain's gig, in which Bob and his friends had left the ill-fated *Eagle*.

"Do you think there'll be anything left in her?" asked Bob.

"There will, unless she is smashed," replied Mr. Spark. "The lockers, in which most of the supplies were packed, are water-tight and securely fastened. This is a piece of good luck, if the boat is not stove in. She has turned bottom up, but she may still be sound. She'll soon be here."

When the gig was close enough so that they could wade out to it, Bob and Tim Flynn rolled up their trousers and went through the shallow surf. The beach gradually shelved at this point and they could wade out nearly a quarter of a mile at low tide.

"She's all right, cap'n!" called the sailor, when he and Bob reached the small craft. "Sound as a dollar, and the lockers are closed," he added as the boat rolled partly over.

"Good!" cried the commander. "Pull her in as close as you can and we'll unload her. Then we'll get her above high-water mark. This boat may save our lives."

"How?" asked Mr. Tarbill.

"Why, when the sea goes down we can leave the island in her."

"Leave the island? Never! I'm on dry land now, and I'm never going to trust myself in a boat again."

"Maybe you'll think differently after a bit," said the captain.

By this time Bob and Tim had the boat in very shallow water. They managed to turn it on the keel, and the first thing they saw was the sail in the bottom. Ropes, fastened to various projections, had prevented the canvas from floating away.

"There!" cried the captain, when he saw it. "That solves our shelter problem for us. We'll make a tent. Oh, we're in luck, all right. 'Bob's Island' isn't such a bad place after all."

Bob blushed with pleasure. Then and there he made up his mind that his foolishness should be a thing of the past. He was of some importance in the world now, and it would not do to be playing childish pranks.

But if the captain was delighted at finding the sail, he was much more so when, on opening the lockers, which fastened with patent catches, everything was found to be as "dry as a bone," as Tim Flynn expressed it.

"Now we can have a change from the fish and fruit diet," said the captain, as he showed where the canned food had been stowed away. There were tins of ship's biscuits, some jars of jam and marmalade, plenty of canned beef, tongue and other meats, rice, flour—in short, a bountiful supply for the small party of castaways.

Captain Spark had ordered the boats to be well provisioned when he knew the *Eagle* was doomed, and his forethought now stood them in good stead.

Frank V. Webster

In another locker was a kit of carpenter's tools, which would come in very handy if they were to remain long on the island, and in another water-tight compartment the captain had stowed his chronometer, his instruments for finding the position of the ship, and some charts.

Owing to the fact that the lockers remained tightly closed when the boat capsized, nothing had been lost out of them, and they had also served to make the gig more buoyant. Practically nothing was missing from the boat save the personal belongings of Bob and the others—their clothing in the valises, the mast which had floated away, and some of the captain's papers relating to the ship. But this did not worry them, as they were now in good shape to live on the island, at least for several weeks.

"All hands to lighten ship!" called the captain, when he had looked over what the boat contained. They made short work of carrying the things from the lockers well up on the beach. With the boat thus made lighter, it was pulled out of reach of the waves.

"Now for a shelter!" the commander called, when the gig had been safely moored. "This sail will make a fine tent."

So it proved when it was set up on some poles which Tim Flynn cut with a light hatchet found among the tools. Mr. Tarbill could not be depended on to do anything, and he was so mournful, standing around and lamenting the fact that he had ever undertaken the trip, that, to get rid of him, Captain Spark sent him off once more to catch turtles, or, if he could not do that, to gather some of the eggs. This last Mr. Tarbill was able to do, but he was not successful in turning any of the crawling creatures over on their backs.

The tent was erected before dark, and, with a cheerful fire burning in front of it, supper was prepared. This time they had tin dishes to eat from, as a supply was found in the gig's lockers.

Tired out with their day's work, and by the struggle with the sea, the castaways all slept soundly. Nor was there any need to stand guard during the night. On beds of palm leaves, under the tent, they slumbered undisturbed until the sun, shining in on them, awoke all four.

"Well, I'm beginning to feel quite to home," remarked the captain, who could be cheerful under misfortune. His good spirits should have been a lesson to Mr. Tarbill. That gentleman had lost nothing but what could be easily replaced, but the captain had lost his fine ship. Still he did not complain, and Bob, seeing his demeanor under trying circumstances, resolved to try and be like the stanch mariner.

After breakfast Captain Spark looked carefully over the gig to see if the craft was seaworthy. He decided that it was, and he sent Tim to look about for a suitable small tree to be cut down as a mast for the sail.

"Are you going to sail away?" asked Mr. Tarbill nervously.

"I don't know. I want to be all ready to do so in case we find it necessary. This noon I will work out our position and locate this island on the chart. Then I can determine how far it is to the nearest mainland, or to a larger island."

"I'll never go in a small boat on this big ocean," declared Mr. Tarbill.

Captain Spark, who had completed his examination of the gig, was standing near it, idly gazing off across the waste of water, which had greatly subsided since the storm, when he caught sight of some small object about two miles off shore.

"Bob!" he called, "bring me the binoculars," for a pair of marine glasses had been found in one of the lockers.

The captain gazed through the glasses for several seconds. Then he cried out:

"More arrivals! Prepare for company, Bob!"

"Who, captain?"

"There's a boat off there and in it are Mr. Carr, the first mate, and Ned Scudd! But they seem to be in trouble, for they are bailing fast. Their boat must have a hole in it. We'd better go to their rescue!"

# CHAPTER XXII

## AFLOAT ONCE MORE

Captain Spark laid aside his binoculars and began shoving the gig down toward the line of surf. The tide was about half in.

"Lend a hand!" cried the commander to Mr. Tarbill. There was no need to urge Bob, who had already grasped one side of the gunwale and was helping to push the boat down the beach.

It was almost too much for the captain and Bob, as Mr. Tarbill, however willing he was, could not bring much strength to the work. Fortunately, however, Tim Flynn came from the woods at that moment, dragging after him a long thin pole to serve as a mast. He saw what the captain wanted and ran up to help. Between the three they managed to get the gig afloat.

"Now then! Lively!" cried the commander. "Their boat is settling fast!"

Tim did not need to be told what the object was in launching the gig. Fortunately there had been a spare pair of oars in the craft when she came ashore, the big blades being fastened so they could not float away. With these the captain and Tim began to propel the boat toward the sinking craft in which were Mr. Carr and Ned Scudd. The two latter were bailing so fast that they had no chance to row. Bob also went in the gig, but Mr. Tarbill remained on shore, nervously running up and down, wringing his hands and uttering vain wishes that he had

Frank V. Webster

never undertaken a sea voyage for his health.

It was not long before the gig was close to the other boat, and Captain Spark called out a glad greeting to his first mate and the sailor.

"What happened?" he asked.

"We hit some floating wreckage last night," explained Mr. Carr. "Stove quite a hole, but I managed to stuff part of a sail in it, and we did very well until early this morning. Then some of the seams began to open, and we're filling fast."

"I'll take you aboard," said the commander. "We've got a nice little island waiting for you. Where are the other men?"

"Drowned," replied Mr. Carr solemnly. "That is, those who were with me. When we got the hole in us they became frightened and leaped overboard—that is, all but Ned here. I tried to make 'em stay in, but they wouldn't. That is the last I saw of them. The other boat, with Sam Bender and his crew, we lost sight of."

"Poor fellows," murmured the captain.

The first mate and Ned were soon in the captain's gig, and shortly afterward the boat with the hole in her filled and sank.

"Never mind," consoled the captain. "It's shallow here and at low tide we may be able to get her. Anything left in her, Mr. Carr?"

"Considerable provisions in the water-tight compartments. Also some supplies."

"Very good. We'll need 'em all. We're quite a party of castaways now."

"How did you find Bob?" asked the first mate, for his boat had been near when the boy fell overboard.

"Oh, Bob discovered the island for us," replied the commander, and he explained the various happenings.

Shore was soon reached, and then Mr. Carr and Ned, neither of whom had been able to eat much because of the necessity of bailing to keep from sinking, were given a good meal.

The two latest arrivals looked with interest on what had already been done to form a camp. When their wet trousers were hung up to dry in the hot sun, they rested in the shade of the tent and Bob explained his adventures on first reaching the island.

"Have you any idea where we are, captain?" asked Mr. Carr, after a mutual exchange of experiences.

"Only a slight one. I'm going to take an observation this noon. Fortunately, my chronometer did not stop and I can get the correct reckoning."

But the captain was disappointed. At noon the sun was hidden under a dense bank of clouds, and, as "dead reckoning" would have been of no avail, since they had no previous record to go by, he had to postpone matters.

However, there was plenty to do. When the tide went out late that afternoon they saw that it would he possible to get most of the things from the wrecked boat. This kept them busy until dark. Then a big campfire was lighted, and, though the tent was rather crowded with six in it, they managed to sleep fairly comfortably.

The next day it rained, and the castaways put in rather a miserable existence. Fortunately, they had carried the food into the tent, where it was protected from the terrific tropical downpour. The rain kept up for three days, and during all that time Mr. Tarbill never ceased complaining.

As for Bob and the others, they did not mind getting wet through, for the weather was very warm. Under the captain's directions they had built a sort of screen for the fire at the first sign of a storm, making it of green cocoanut tree leaves on slanting poles like a "lean-to," and this kept the blaze going in spite of the wetness, as plenty of dry wood had been gathered before the rain began.

On the fourth day the sun shone brightly, the downpour had ceased, and they rejoiced in the beautiful scenery around them, even though they were shipwrecked and on a strange island.

"We must build a more substantial shelter than the tent," Captain Spark decided that morning. "We may have to stay here for several months, and the tent is not large enough. Besides, we must keep our supplies dry."

They decided to make a small log cabin, and, with this end in view, Bob, the two sailors, and Mr. Carr set off into the woods to hew down trees for this purpose.

Captain Spark and Mr. Tarbill remained behind to get the camp in better shape after the storm. The commander also wished to take a sun observation that noon and work out the position of the island,

As Bob and his three companions were going through the wood, they were surprised to see several birds of brilliant plumage. Some of them sang sweetly.

"That's a good sign!" exclaimed Mr. Carr.

"Why?" asked Bob.

"Because if there are birds on this small island, it shows that there must be a larger island not far away. Birds of this kind live in large forests, and as there are none here, on account of the size of this island, that shows they must come from some other one, or from the mainland."

"I hope you're right," said Bob. "We might be able to get to some other island in the gig, and then we would stand a better chance of being rescued."

When the little party got back to camp, carrying a number of poles for the beginning of the hut, they found Captain Spark preparing to take an observation, as it was nearly noon. He asked Mr. Carr to assist him.

In a few minutes, after taking the altitude of the sun through the sextant and working out a calculation from his table of figures, the captain was able to announce the result, giving the latitude and longitude of the island.

"Why," exclaimed Bob, "that is about the location of the island shown on the parchment map that Captain Obed gave me."

"So it is!" cried the captain. "Where is the map, Bob?"

"Lost overboard with the rest of my things, I suppose, when the boat capsized," was the rueful answer.

"That's so. Now we'll never know whether there was any treasure or not. However, there's no use worrying about that. The best news is that we are not far off from a very large island, at which ships frequently touch for water and provisions."

"Good!" cried Mr. Carr. "About how far off, captain?"

"Not more than two hundred miles."

"But how can we go two hundred miles?" asked Mr. Tarbill.

"In the small boat—my gig—to be sure. We have sufficient provisions for twice that journey, and the boat is large enough,"

"I'll never venture to sea in a small boat!" declared the nervous passenger.

The others paid little attention to him, being too much interested in what the captain had to say about the other island. He had never been there, but he had heard of it. It was inhabited by a tribe of friendly natives.

"Shall we start soon?" asked Mr. Carr.

"I think we'll wait a week or two and see what turns up here. We are very comfortable, and I don't want to undertake the voyage in the small boat if there is any chance of a ship taking us off from here."

The thought that they were not so very far from an island, where the chances of rescue were most excellent, put every one in good humor, save Mr. Tarbill. He remained gloomy and nervous.

It was decided to proceed with the building of the hut, and in a few days it was finished and thatched with thick green leaves, that were almost as good as shingles.

"There, now let it rain if it wants to," said Mr. Carr. "We'll be good and dry. The tent can be used as a storehouse for what the hut won't hold."

It seemed as if the rain was going to take them at their word, for there came a steady downpour the next day, and it lasted a week with but few intermissions. They were very weary of it.

Yet through it all Bob kept up his good spirits. He was a changed boy, and though, once or twice, the spirit of mischief seemed about to break out in him, he restrained it, to the secret delight of Captain Spark.

"I was right, after all," he said to Mr. Carr, one day when the rain had ceased. "It needed a sea voyage to straighten Bob out, but I didn't figure on a shipwreck doing it."

The boy was very helpful about camp. No task was too hard for him, no labor too much, and he never grumbled. He had grown almost used to life on the island, as had the other castaways. But Captain Spark had not given up the plan of sailing for the large island. He waited until he thought the weather had settled down and then, one fine morning, he gave the word to load the small boat with all their supplies.

"Do you think we can make it?" asked Mr. Carr.

"I think so. We can try, at any rate. We'll have this island and the log cabin to return to in case we have to turn back."

"Are you really going to put to sea in that small boat?" asked Mr. Tarbill nervously, when the time for departure came.

"That's what we are," replied the captain.

"Then I'm not going."

"Very well. If you want to stay we'll leave you some provisions, and perhaps, in six months, a ship may pass here and see the shirt signal."

"Six months?"

"Well, maybe longer; maybe a shorter time."

"And I'll have to stay here all alone?"

"That's what you will," answered Captain Spark shortly, for he was beginning to tire of Mr. Tarbill's cowardice.

"Oh, dear! What shall I do?" exclaimed the nervous man.

"Come along with us," suggested Bob.

Frank V. Webster

"I'm afraid."

"Then stay on the island. That won't sink," said the captain.

"I'm afraid of that, too."

"Well, we're going," announced the commander, preparing to aid in shoving the boat down to the water's edge.

"Oh! Don't leave me behind! I'll go! I'll go! But I know I'll be drowned! I'm sure of it!"

"You're a cheerful passenger," murmured the captain, as Mr. Tarbill got into the boat. "Let her go, boys!"

A few minutes later they were afloat once more, leaving "Bob's Island" behind. Would they be able to reach the other one! That was the question in every heart.

# CHAPTER XXIII

## A SERIOUS LOSS

Under a bright blue sky, with the sun shining down almost a little too warm for comfort, and with the sea very calm, the voyage that meant so much to all of them was begun. They looked back with a little regret at the small island they were leaving. There, at least, they knew they would be safe, but unless they desired to risk the chance of staying there many months, they must make this venture.

"Well, it was a fine little camp," murmured Bob, with a tone of sorrow in his voice.

"Indeed it was," declared Mr. Tarbill. "I wish I was back there now."

"Perhaps we all will be," said Captain Spark gravely, "but there is no use discovering a leak in your boat until it's actually there," which was his way of saying that it was bad luck to cross a bridge until you came to it.

"Now we've got to have some system about this voyage," went on the commander. "We've got enough provisions and water to last us for the trip if we are careful of them. We'll not be able to have any banquets, and I depend upon every one—in which I include myself—to be sparing of the food and drink. There is no telling what may happen."

"I have a very good appetite since taking this sea voyage," murmured Mr. Tarbill. "I can't bear to think of being hungry."

"Well, perhaps there'll be no need for it. I only wanted to warn you. Now I propose to take command of this gig, for it is my property, and I'm going to be obeyed, just as if we were on the *Eagle*."

"Aye, aye, sir," replied the sailors promptly.

"I'll do my best to bring the craft to the larger island as soon as possible. We'll have to depend somewhat on the wind, for we can't row all that distance in time to make our provisions last. Fortunately, I have a reliable pocket compass, so I can lay our course fairly accurately. Now, Ned Scudd and Tim Flynn, step the mast and hoist the sail and we'll see how our craft behaves under canvas."

The two sailors soon had the sail hoisted, and under the influence of a stiff breeze the gig shot rapidly ahead, the oars being shipped. They had two pairs now, one the spare lot from the gig and the other from the boat Mr. Carr had commanded.

Captain Spark arranged his pocket compass on the stern seat near the tiller, and sitting there he directed the course of the small boat as nearly as he could toward the large island. He and Mr. Carr were to divide the watches of the day and night. There would be four, of six hours each. That is, Captain Spark would be in charge of the boat for six hours, and then Mr. Carr would go on watch for the same length of time, until it became the captain's turn again. In this way each one could get sufficient rest.

The two sailors, Bob and Mr. Tarbill were divided between the two heads of the watch, Bob and Tim Flynn being chosen by the captain.

The food had been carefully stowed away in the lockers, the captain's charts, chronometer and sextant were put where he could easily get at them, and as they had breakfasted before they set off on their voyage, there was nothing to do for several hours but to make themselves as comfortable as possible in the boat.

Had it not been for the worry over what might be the outcome, and had not the dreadful memory of the shipwreck been in all their minds, they might have enjoyed the sail. As it was, no one felt very jolly. Mr. Tarbill was particularly miserable, and was continually finding fault.

"Oh, dear! It's dreadfully hot!" he exclaimed when they had been sailing for several hours and Bob's Island was out of sight. "I'm afraid I shall be sunstruck."

"Get in the shadow of the sail. Go forward," advised Captain Spark.

"I'm afraid to move for fear I'll slip overboard as Bob did."

"Well, if you do we can see to fish you out. It's daylight now."

"Oh, I'm miserable! I wish I had never come on this trip! I know I shall never live to see home again!"

"I, too, wish you hadn't come," thought the captain, but he really felt sorry for the nervous man.

Finally it grew so hot that Mr. Tarbill could stand it no longer. He decided he would make his way forward, where he could be in the shade of the sail. The others were very warm also, but they did not complain. Even Bob, who was not used to roughing it as were the sailors, stood it bravely, though the hot sun made his head ache.

Mr. Tarbill, who was in the stern, near Captain Spark, arose and started forward. As he did so a wave, larger than any that the boat had previously encountered, careened the craft a bit.

Frank V. Webster

"Oh, I'm going overboard!" exclaimed Mr. Tarbill.

He made a frantic clutch at the air, and really did almost go over the side, but it was due more to his own awkwardness than to anything else. Then he slipped down into the bottom of the gig, but as he did so his arm shot out and something bright and shining was knocked from the after locker over the gunwale into the sea, where it fell with a little splash.

"Now you have done it!" cried the captain, standing up and making a vain grab.

"Done it? Done what?" asked Mr. Tarbill.

"You've knocked overboard the only compass we had! How we're going to find the island now is more than I can tell! This is a serious loss."

# CHAPTER XXIV

## DAYS OF HOPELESSNESS

The captain's announcement struck terror to every heart. Even Bob, with the little knowledge of the sea he possessed, realized what that meant. They would have to "go it blind" now, and the chances of finding a comparatively small island in that vast ocean were little indeed.

"Did I knock the compass overboard?" asked Mr. Tarbill.

"You certainly did," spoke the captain grimly.

"I—I didn't mean to."

"No, I don't suppose you did. Still, it's on the bottom of the ocean by this time."

"Oh, dear! What shall we do?"

"The best we can. Fortunately, I have a general idea of the direction of our course, and at night I can make a shift to steer by the stars, but it's going to be pretty much guesswork."

"If we can't find the big island, can't we go back to the small one where we were?" asked Bob hopefully.

"It would be about as hard to find that as it's going to be to locate the other now. Still, we'll have to do the best we can. It's your watch, Mr. Carr. Keep her as near as you can about as she is while this wind holds. We'll have a bit to eat now."

The captain dealt out the food and the supply of water. The amount of the latter was very small, as they did not have many casks in which to store a supply for their voyage. Still, no one complained, even Mr. Tarbill being too stunned by what he had done to find any fault.

The day passed slowly, and the breeze kept up. But whether they were being urged on toward the island, or whether the wind had shifted and was bearing them in another direction, was something no one could tell. A deeper gloom than any that had prevailed since the shipwreck fell upon them all.

When it got dark and the stars came out Captain Spark was able to direct the boat to a little better advantage, but when morning came, after the long darkness, during which no one had slept well, they found themselves on a vast, heaving expanse of water.

"Where are we?" asked Mr. Tarbill. "Is the island in sight?"

Captain Spark swept the horizon with his glasses.

"There's not a sail to be seen," he said, "and no sign of land. I thought we would raise the island by this morning."

"Then don't you know where we are?" asked the nervous man.

"I haven't the least idea, except that we are somewhere on the Pacific Ocean."

The captain spoke rather hopelessly.

"Never mind," said Bob cheerfully. "We've got food enough for a week, and by that time something may happen."

"Yes, something may," said Mr. Carr, with a gloomy look.

"That's the way to talk, Bob," exclaimed the captain. "Never say die. We'll cheat old Davy Jones and his locker yet."

Indeed, Bob's cheerfulness under trying circumstances was something that the captain had marked with satisfaction. The very character of the boy had undergone a change because of what he had been through. He seemed to have grown older and to have a fitting idea of responsibility. Bob was beginning to realize that life was not all play.

It was rather hopeless sailing now, not knowing whether they were headed right or not. Still they kept on. They ate all they wanted, for the food was more plentiful than water, and they knew if worst came to worst they could live for several days without victuals, but not without water.

Slowly the time dragged on. Nobody aboard the craft knew what to do. Once Bob tried to cheer up and hum a ditty, but the effort was a dismal failure.

"Bob, I reckon you are sorry now that you left home and came with me," observed the captain soberly.

"I'm not sorry that I left home," answered the lad promptly. "But I must confess I am sorry that all of us are in such a pickle as this."

"If I had known my ship was going to be wrecked I'd not have taken you on this voyage."

"It is an awful loss."

"Yes—but I sha'n't mind it so much, if only we reach a place of safety."

"Oh, if only I was home!" sighed Mr. Tarbill. "If only I was home!"

"Wouldn't just dry land suit you?" queried Bob, with a bit of his old-time humor.

"I—I suppose so, but I'd like home best."

"Any land would suit me just now," put in the captain.

"Supposing we should land among cannibals!" murmured the nervous passenger.

"I don't believe there are any around here," answered Captain Spark.

"But are you sure?"

"No, I am not sure."

"I knew it! Oh, if the savages got us it would be terrible!" And Mr. Tarbill shuddered.

"Well, he's a wet blanket, if ever there was one!" declared Mr. Carr, in deep disgust.

"I am—er—a wet blanket?" demanded the nervous passenger.

"Yes, you are!" declared the other. "And I, for one, am tired of hearing you croak."

"Hum!" murmured Mr. Tarbill, and then, for the time being, he said no more. The constant rocking of the boat made him somewhat sick at the stomach, and he was anything but happy.

Bob could not help but think of home, and of his dear mother and father. If he was lost, what would they say and what would they do?

"Dear folks at home!" he murmured. "If I ever get back you'll find me a different boy, yes, indeed, you will! No more silly tricks for Bob!" And he shut his lips with a firmness that meant a great deal.

The boy had just closed his eyes to take a nap when a loud cry from Tim Flynn awoke him.

"What's the matter?" he questioned.

"What do you see, Tim?" asked the captain.

The sailor was at the bow, standing up on the seat and gazing far across the rising and falling waters. He did not answer until the craft was on the crest of a high wave.

"A ship!" he exclaimed.

"Where?" came from all of the others in concert.

"Dead ahead!"

Both the captain and Mr. Carr looked and saw that the report was true. Far, far away could be seen a low-lying dark object, with a trail of smoke behind it.

"It's a steamer," said Captain Spark.

"Is it headed this way?" asked Bob, eagerly.

"I believe so."

"Are you sure, sir?" came from Mr. Tarbill. "Please don't make any mistake."

"No, I am not sure. Tim, what do you think?" went on the captain.

The sailor shrugged his shoulders. He was too anxious to even venture an opinion.

How eagerly all on board the little craft watched that dark object so far away! One minute they felt certain the steamer was headed toward them, the next they were afraid it was moving off to the northward.

"Let's sail after the steamer," suggested Bob.

"It won't help us much," answered Mr. Carr.

"Never mind, it will help some," came from Captain Spark, and they sailed and rowed with all the skill and strength they possessed.

"Are we closer?" asked Mr. Tarbill.

"Not yet!" answered the captain.

"Can't we call to them?"

"No—but we can fire a shot," answered Captain Spark, and not one shot but half a dozen were discharged.

"If only the lookout sees us," said Bob. "I wish we could hoist some big signal."

But they had nothing larger than the sail and a shirt. Mr. Carr furnished the garment and it was tied to the masthead. But if those on the steamer saw the signal they gave no sign.

"She's goin' away!" wailed Tim Flynn at last. "Bad luck to her fer lavin' us!"

"Going away!" ejaculated Bob, and his heart sank like a lump of lead in his bosom.

"Don't say that!" wailed Mr. Tarbill. "Shout—fire a gun—anything! They must come and rescue us!" And in his nervousness the man began to caper about wildly.

"Look out, or you'll go overboard!" shouted Captain Spark.

Scarcely had he spoken when the boat was caught by a big

wave and stood up almost on end. With a yell Mr. Tarbill slid to the stern, clutched at the gunwale, and disappeared with a splash.

"Man overboard!"

"Of all the fools!" muttered Mr. Carr. "Why couldn't he sit still and behave himself?" His patience, so far as the nervous passenger was concerned, was completely exhausted.

Bob reached for the boathook, and as soon as Mr. Tarbill came up, he caught the iron in the man's coat and hauled him to the side. Then the captain and Tim Flynn hauled him back on board.

"Help! I am drowning! Save me!" spluttered the nervous passenger. "I'll go to the bottom of the Pacific!"

"No, you won't," answered Captain Spark. "But after this you had better sit still."

"Oh, what a trying experience!" wailed the unfortunate one. He cleared his mouth of water. "Why did you let me go overboard?" he demanded. "Why didn't you stop me when you saw me slipping?"

"Didn't have time," answered the captain. "You ought to thank Bob for hooking you."

"He tore my coat sleeve," said Mr. Tarbill, examining the garment. "And it's the only coat I have now," he added mournfully.

"Never mind, maybe you won't need a coat soon," put in Mr. Carr, who was more disgusted than ever.

"How's that?"

"If we go down the fish won't care if we have coats on or

not—guess they'd rather eat us without coats."

"Oh dear! Oh dear!" gasped the nervous passenger, and then he all but collapsed.

"The steamer is turning!" cried Tim Flynn, who had climbed up the mast to obtain a better view. "Good luck to her if she comes this way!"

"If only we could send her a wireless message!" said Bob.

"Yes, here is where that newfangled telegraphing would come in handy," returned Captain Spark. "But we ain't got no apparatus, so we can't do it."

With anxious eyes all watched the big steamer, which looked to be steering almost for them. The craft was a long way off, so they could make out nothing distinctly.

"It's clouding down—we are going to have a squall!" cried Captain Spark suddenly.

He pointed to the eastward and the others saw that he was right. As if by magic dark clouds were rolling up from the horizon. The wind died out, and then came in uncertain puffs.

"The steamer is leaving us!" cried Mr. Carr.

"Oh, don't say that, please don't!" wailed Mr. Tarbill.

"Here comes the squall!" cried Captain Spark, and he was right.

Soon a sudden gust of wind struck the sailboat, almost keeling her over. As quickly as it could be done, the sail was lowered and stowed away.

The squall was of short duration, lasting all told not more than ten minutes. Only a few drops of rain fell. Then the clouds rolled off to the westward and it became as clear as before.

"The steamer! It's gone!" shouted Mr. Carr.

"What!" cried Captain Spark.

"Gone, I tell you!"

With great anxiety all strained their eyes to catch some sight of the large craft. At last Tim Flynn pointed with his finger.

"There she is—sailin' right away from us!" he said bitterly.

The words of the Irish tar proved true—the steamer had again altered her course. In a few minutes her dark form was swallowed up in the distant haze.

It must be admitted that all were much cast down by this happening. When the steamer had headed directly for them they had thought sure they would be rescued.

"They must have done it deliberately," said Mr. Tarbill. "Oh, the villains! the scoundrels!"

"I don't believe that," answered Captain Spark. "More'n likely they didn't see us. No captain would be so inhuman as to pass us by."

Two hours dragged by slowly. Tim Flynn was tired out with much watching and had lain down and Ned Scudd had taken his place.

"I see something," said Ned, presently. "Don't know what it is."

He pointed to the southward. There was some low-lying object, with the waves dashing against it.

"Perhaps it's a ship with the masts gone," said Mr. Carr.

"Or a dead whale," suggested Bob.

"It's too big for either a ship or a whale," said the captain. "Let us sail toward it and make an inspection."

"Don't—don't run into any new danger!" pleaded Mr. Tarbill.

"Anything is better than to remain out on this dreary waste of waters," answered Mr. Carr.

The castaways turned their boat in the direction of the distant object. It was further off than they had anticipated, and as they slowly approached they made out a long, low-lying island, covered with bushes and grass. Over the island hovered myriads of birds.

"An island!" cried Bob. "Now we can go ashore anyhow!"

"Not much of a place, I am afraid," answered Captain Spark, slowly taking in the spot from end to end with his sharp eyes.

"Well, it's better nor nuthin," came from Tim Flynn. "Sure, an' some av thim burds will make good eatin', so they will!"

"We want to be careful how we go ashore," cautioned the captain. "We don't want to damage our boat."

They approached the new land cautiously. The water all around it seemed to be deep, so there was no danger of striking a hidden reef.

Presently the captain espied a sandy beach, and straight for this the craft was headed. As the boat struck, Bob, Tim and Ned leaped out, followed by Mr. Carr, and, aided by the swells, pulled her well up.

"Am I—er—to get out?" asked Mr. Tarbill timidly.

"As you please," answered Captain Spark, grimly. "I am going ashore."

"Then I'll go, too—I don't want to be left alone," said the nervous passenger.

Soon all were on the beach, and then the boat was dragged higher up still, and tied to several of the low trees near by.

"Let me shoot some birds—they will make fine eating," said Bob to the captain, and permission being given, the young castaway went on a brief hunt. The birds were so thick that he had little difficulty in bringing down several dozen.

"Now we can have a bird pot-pie for supper," declared Mr. Carr, and he looked greatly pleased, and so did the others.

All realized that the island upon which they had landed was not to be compared to that upon which they had previously been cast. The trees were of small account, none of them bearing fruit fit to eat. Some of the bushes contained berries, and Ned began to gather a cupful.

"Go slow there, Ned," said the captain. "They may be poisonous."

"They can't be—for I saw the birds feeding on, them," said Bob.

"Oh, well, then it is all right."

But the berries proved rather bitter to the taste and nobody felt like eating many of them. Tim started a fire, and over this they broiled and roasted the birds, each fixing the evening meal in the way that best suited him.

"Are there any cannibals here?" asked Mr. Tarbill.

"I don't believe there is a soul on the island besides ourselves," answered the captain.

"I can't go to sleep if there are cannibals," groaned the nervous passenger.

As late as it was, Bob, Ned and the captain took a tramp around the island. It was not over a quarter of a mile long and an eighth of a mile wide. There was fairly good walking close to the shore, but the interior was a mass of stunted trees, thorny bushes and long trailing vines, to get through which was impossible.

"I haven't seen what I'd like most to see," said the captain, after the walk was ended.

"What is that?" questioned Bob.

"A spring of good, fresh water."

"That's so—we didn't see any spring at all!" exclaimed Ned Scudd. "Too bad! We need water."

The castaways were thoroughly tired out, and that night all went to bed and slept soundly. Nothing came to disturb them, although at daybreak Mr. Tarbill leaped up in alarm.

"Hark!" he cried. "Somebody is coming! It must be the cannibals!"

"What!" exclaimed Captain Spark, and he jumped up, followed by the others.

Then all listened. From the interior of the little island came a most unearthly screaming.

"Somebody is being murdered!" gasped Mr. Tarbill, and sank on his knees. "Oh, oh, why did I leave home!"

They listened intently, and then Mr. Carr set up a laugh.

"What is it?" asked Bob, curiously.

"Parrots, my boy, nothing but parrots."

"To be sure—I should have knowed it," came from the captain. "They allers screech like that in the morning."

"Are you sure they are parrots?" asked the nervous passenger.

"Dead certain," answered Mr. Carr. "If you don't believe it, just go over to yonder trees and shoo them up into the air."

"I—I don't think I care to do that—they might fly at me and peck me."

"Well, they are parrots—and they won't hurt you if you leave 'em alone."

During the morning the search for a spring of water was resumed. At last they found several pools, the water coming up in them from underground. But the birds used the pools for drinking places and they were consequently far from clean.

"How long are we to stay on this island?" asked Mr. Tarbill, while they were eating a breakfast of broiled birds, fish, and crackers.

"Not very long, I'm thinking," answered the captain. "In a storm it wouldn't be a very safe place. The water must sweep the land pretty well, and our boat would be stove to pieces."

"But where are you going?"

"We'll try to make that big island I spoke about," went on the captain. Then of a sudden, he bent closer to the nervous man. "What's that on your watch chain?" he demanded,

"My watch chain?"

"Yes. It looks like a tiny compass to me."

"Why—er—it is a compass," stammered Mr. Tarbill.

"And you never told us that you had it!" roared the captain.

"I—I forgot it!" stammered the passenger. "I—I was so upset, you know."

"Let me see it."

Captain Spark took the compass and examined it with care. It was small, but of good manufacture, and looked as if it might point true.

"Not near as good as the one we lost," he said to Mr. Carr. "But it is better than nothing."

"Indeed it is," was the reply.

"I thought that was a locket," said Bob. "I noticed it on the watch chain several times."

"It was given to me by my uncle, years ago," said Mr. Tarbill. "Please don't lose it."

"I'll keep it safe, don't fear," answered the captain. "Reckon it is safer in my keepin' than yours," he added.

With the discovery of the tiny compass the hopes of the castaways revived. All felt that it would be a waste of time to remain on the small island, and accordingly preparations were made to leave on the following morning. To add to their stock of provisions the men and Bob brought down a large quantity of birds and also caught a lot of fish, and these were broiled and cooked, to keep them from spoiling. They also got what water they could and stored it in a cask, and Bob picked a capful of berries.

"Some of the parrots are beautiful," said the boy to the captain. "If I was sure of getting home again I'd like to take some of the feathers along, for my mother's hat."

"Better not bother, Bob."

"I'll not. I was only thinking, sir."

"I have great hopes of reaching that large island," went on Captain Spark. "But, when we embark again, we'll have to take what comes. That little compass will help us some, but it may not be as accurate as is necessary."

"Why not stay on this island till a ship comes along?"

"I don't consider this as safe as the other island was."

That night Bob went to bed early. He awoke in the middle of the night to feel somebody or something pulling at his foot.

"Hi! who is there?" he shouted, sitting up. At the same moment came a wild yell from Mr. Tarbill.

"The cannibals have come!" yelled the nervous man. "One of 'em has me by the throat!"

"Stop that row!" came from Captain Spark. "There are no savages here!"

"Maybe he's got the nightmare," suggested Mr. Carr.

"No, no, I am attacked!" bawled Mr. Tarbill.

"I know what they are!" shouted Bob. "Get out of here, you imp!" And he struck something with a stick that was handy. There was a wild chattering and off into the darkness stole several impish figures.

"What were they?" asked Ned, who was still sleepy.

"Monkeys," answered the youth, "Pretty big ones, too."

"Are you sure they weren't cannibals?" queried Mr. Tarbill. "Some of the wild men are very small, you know. In Africa they are not over three feet high."

"Monkeys, true enough," said the captain. "I saw some of 'em watching our camp when we had supper. They were afraid to come close when we were stirring, but I suppose when we were quiet their curiosity got the best of them, and they had to come and feel of us."

"Ugh! I don't want any more of them to come near me," said Mr. Tarbill, with a shudder.

The weather was all that could be desired, and the captain determined to make the most of it. An early breakfast was had, and then the things were taken back to the boat.

"All aboard!" shouted Captain Spark. "And may we now locate that large island without further trouble."

"Oh, I wish I was home!" groaned Mr. Tarbill.

The boat was floated without difficulty, and the castaways got aboard. They rowed for some distance and then the sail was hoisted. Inside of an hour the little, island faded from their view and once more they found themselves alone on the bosom of the broad Pacific.

The captain had great hopes of the small compass, but he and the others were doomed to disappointment. The compass proved unreliable, as they discovered that night, when the stars came out.

"It's no use," said Captain Spark. "We have got to sail by our wits, if we ever expect to reach a place of safety." And all that day they kept on, not knowing if they were heading in the proper direction or not.

It was just getting dusk of the second day of their voyage, when Tim Flynn, opening a forward locker to set out some things for the evening meal, made a startling discovery.

"The gig has sprung a leak!" he exclaimed.

"A leak!" cried the captain.

"Yes, this locker is half full of water, and all the stuff in it is soaked."

It was true enough. The salt water had come in through some opening of the seams of the previously tight compartment and had done much damage. The victuals were only fit to throw overboard.

"Half rations from now on," said the captain sternly.

"Half rations!" repeated Mr. Tarbill. "Why, I'm awful hungry!"

"And you're liable to be for some days to come," answered the commander. "We'll share and share alike, but every one will have to curb his appetite."

"Oh, this dreadful shipwreck! I wish I had stayed home!"

The others wished the same thing.

It was a night without hope, and the morning broke dull and gray, with the promise of a storm. The wind shifted from point to point until the castaways did not know in which direction they were going, for there was no sun to guide them. The leaky locker was tightly closed, so that there was no danger of the boat filling from it.

The amount of breakfast seemed woefully small to Bob, and he recalled with a start the wish Dent Freeman, the hired man, had expressed, that the boy who tormented him would have to eat seaweed.

"Perhaps I shall before we're through with this," said the lad to himself. "There isn't much more food left."

Still he did not complain, setting a good example in this respect to Mr. Tarbill, who did nothing but find fault, until Captain Spark ordered him to take an oar and with one of the sailors aid in propelling the boat, for the wind had suddenly died out.

For two days more they sailed or rowed on.

The weather continued unsettled, but fortunately not breaking into a storm. Sometimes there was a breeze, and again there was a dead calm, when they took turns at the oars. It was all guesswork as to whether or not they were headed for the island.

The food became less and less, until finally they were living on three dry biscuits a day each. The water, too, was getting lower and lower in the one cask that remained, and it had a warm, brackish taste. Still it was the most precious thing they possessed.

More and more worried became the look on Captain Spark's face. How anxiously each morning and a dozen times a day did he scan the horizon with his glasses for a sight of the island or a ship! But nothing was to be seen save the heaving billows.

Mr. Tarbill became weak-minded, and babbled of cooling streams of water and delicious food until Ned Scudd, losing all patience, threatened to throw the nervous man overboard if he did not cease. This had the effect of quieting him for a while.

The faces of all were haggard and thin. Their eyes were unnaturally bright. Poor Bob bore up bravely, though tears came into his eyes as he thought of his father and mother, and the pleasant and happy home now so far away.

"Bob's as good as a man," whispered the captain to Mr. Carr, and the first mate nodded an assent.

It was the third day of absolute hopelessness. The water was reduced to so little that only a small cupful could be served to each one as the day's supply. Enough biscuits for two days remained. They had lost all sense of direction, for a fog obscured the sun.

On the morning of the fourth day Bob awoke from a troubled sleep to find Mr. Carr dozing at the helm. There was no need to steer, for there had been a dead calm for many hours, and they did not row during the night.

Bob's tongue felt like a piece of rubber in his mouth. His throat was parched and dry, and his stomach craved woefully for food. He stood up on a forward locker, and, taking the captain's glasses, slowly swept them around the sky-line.

Was it imagination, or did he really see some small black object off to the left? His heart beat fast, and his nerves were throbbing so he could not hold the glasses steady.

Captain Spark roused himself from a brief nap. He saw what Bob was doing.

"See anything?" he asked listlessly.

"I don't know—I'm not sure—there's something off there that looks like—"

"Let me take the glasses!" cried the commander.

He fairly snatched them from the boy. With his trained vision he looked long where Bob pointed. Then he cried:

"Thank God! There's a boat coming toward us. I think we're saved! There are natives in it, but they don't seem to have any weapons! I believe they're from the big island. Row, men, row as hard as you can and we'll meet them the sooner!"

Frank V. Webster

Tim and Ned caught up the oars and sent the gig over the calm water at a fast rate of speed.

## CHAPTER XXV

## HOMEWARD BOUND—CONCLUSION

Before an hour had passed the oncoming boat was in plain sight. Then the castaways could see it contained four brown-skinned natives. But, though they were savages, they were not warlike. In fact, they waved their hands in welcome, and called encouragingly to those in the gig.

"I hope they have some water aboard," said Mr. Tarbill. "I'd give anything for some right off the ice."

"I'd be glad of some out of a tea-kettle," said the captain, for the last in the cask had been dealt out some time before.

A little later the commander was exchanging a few words with the natives, as he found he could speak a little of their language.

"We're within a few miles of the big island," he told his anxious companions. "This is a fishing party in one of their big native canoes. They'll show us the way back, and they have plenty of water."

The parched throats and swelling tongues of the castaways were soon relieved by a fairly cool drink from the filled skins in the native boat. Then the brown men passed over some cocoa-nuts and other fruit that were grateful to the palates of the half-starved ones.

Frank V. Webster

Captain Spark conversed a little longer with the friendly savages, and some news they gave him seemed to give him great satisfaction.

"There's an American ship in port at the island," he said, "and she's homeward bound around the Horn. We can take passage in her. Hurrah, men, our troubles seem to be over!"

"Thank God!" said Mr. Carr fervently, and so great was the strain on Mr. Tarbill that when it was relieved by the good news he cried like a child. Nor were Bob's eyes altogether dry.

A little breeze had sprung up, and, guided by the natives, the castaways were soon at the island. It was a large one, and the first sight they had of it showed them a big ship in the harbor. At this they set up a cheer.

It did not take Captain Spark long to arrange matters with the American skipper. He agreed to let the sailors, Bob and Mr. Tarbill work their passage home, and Captain Spark was to give his services as assistant navigator in lieu of passage money.

As the ship was taking on part of a cargo of native produce from the island she was not quite ready to sail, and in the meanwhile Bob and the captain went about the island a bit, Bob collecting a number of curiosities. The natives treated them kindly, and the four who had saved the lives of the castaways by appearing in the nick of time felt well repaid by the present of a few trinkets which Bob and the sailors had in their pockets.

Finally the time came for them to take passage on the *Walrus*, which was the name of the American ship. They sailed one bright morning, and under a spanking breeze the big island was presently low down on the horizon.

Bob was soon a favorite with every one on the ship, he was so anxious to learn and so ready and obliging. He never grumbled, even when the work was hard. But Mr. Tarbill never ceased lamenting the fact that he had ever left home.

As for our hero, he seemed to have settled down in life and was fast learning to become a good sailor. The pranks he used to play were now a thing of the past, and he fully justified the good opinion Captain Spark had of him.

It was a six months' trip home, for they were delayed two weeks or more by contrary winds, and several days longer in making the passage of Magellan Straits.

As the Walrus was to put in at Charleston, South Carolina, it was necessary for Captain Spark, Bob and Mr. Tarbill to make the rest of the journey home by rail. Mr. Carr and the two sailors secured berths in the *Walrus*. Though Captain Spark had lost all his money in the shipwreck, he was able to borrow enough for the fares of himself, Bob and Mr. Tarbill.

Bob reached home a little short of a year from the time he had left. He was a much better boy than when he went away. His father and mother did not need to be told of the change in him. They could see it for themselves.

"What did I tell you?" asked Captain Spark triumphantly of Mrs. Henderson. "I said the voyage would make a man of Bob, and it did."

"The voyage or the shipwreck?" asked Mrs. Henderson.

"I guess it needed both," ventured Bob's father.

Of course Bob was the hero, of all his associates, and they never tired of hearing his stories of what had happened. Later it was learned that Second-Mate Bender and his men had been picked up by a passing vessel and saved. As for Captain Obediah Hickson, when he heard that Bob had returned, he hastened to see him, took him off into a corner and whispered:

"Did ye git th' treasure, Bob?"

"No, captain. I don't believe there was any. We didn't have a chance to look for the island before the shipwreck, and after it the map got lost."

"Well, maybe it's jest as well, Bob," said the old man with a philosophical air. "I'm gittin' too old to need so much money anyhow, an' you're young enough to earn what you need. I reckon it's jest as well," and with a chuckle he shuffled off.

As for Bob, he had such a liking for the sea, in spite of the terrors of the deep, that when he completed his education he became mate on a vessel, and finally captain, and now is in a fair way to become part owner of a big ship trading between New York and South American ports. And here we will say good-by to Bob Henderson, the former castaway.

# Choose from Thousands of 1stWorldLibrary Classics By

A. M. Barnard
Ada Leverson
Adolphus William Ward
Aesop
Agatha Christie
Alexander Aaronsohn
Alexander Kielland
Alexandre Dumas
Alfred Gatty
Alfred Ollivant
Alice Duer Miller
Alice Turner Curtis
Alice Dunbar
Allen Chapman
Alleyne Ireland
Ambrose Bierce
Amelia E. Barr
Amory H. Bradford
Andrew Lang
Andrew McFarland Davis
Andy Adams
Angela Brazil
Anna Alice Chapin
Anna Sewell
Annie Besant
Annie Hamilton Donnell
Annie Payson Call
Annie Roe Carr
Annonaymous
Anton Chekhov
Archibald Lee Fletcher
Arnold Bennett
Arthur C. Benson
Arthur Conan Doyle
Arthur M. Winfield
Arthur Ransome
Arthur Schnitzler
Arthur Train
Atticus
B.H. Baden-Powell
B. M. Bower
B. C. Chatterjee
Baroness Emmuska Orczy
Baroness Orczy
Basil King
Bayard Taylor
Ben Macomber
Bertha Muzzy Bower
Bjornstjerne Bjornson

Booth Tarkington
Boyd Cable
Bram Stoker
C. Collodi
C. E. Orr
C. M. Ingleby
Carolyn Wells
Catherine Parr Traill
Charles A. Eastman
Charles Amory Beach
Charles Dickens
Charles Dudley Warner
Charles Farrar Browne
Charles Ives
Charles Kingsley
Charles Klein
Charles Hanson Towne
Charles Lathrop Pack
Charles Romyn Dake
Charles Whibley
Charles Willing Beale
Charlotte M. Braeme
Charlotte M. Yonge
Charlotte Perkins Stetson
Clair W. Hayes
Clarence Day Jr.
Clarence E. Mulford
Clemence Housman
Confucius
Coningsby Dawson
Cornelis DeWitt Wilcox
Cyril Burleigh
D. H. Lawrence
Daniel Defoe
David Garnett
Dinah Craik
Don Carlos Janes
Donald Keyhoe
Dorothy Kilner
Dougan Clark
Douglas Fairbanks
E. Nesbit
E. P. Roe
E. Phillips Oppenheim
E. S. Brooks
Earl Barnes
Edgar Rice Burroughs
Edith Van Dyne
Edith Wharton

Edward Everett Hale
Edward J. O'Biren
Edward S. Ellis
Edwin L. Arnold
Eleanor Atkins
Eleanor Hallowell Abbott
Eliot Gregory
Elizabeth Gaskell
Elizabeth McCracken
Elizabeth Von Arnim
Ellem Key
Emerson Hough
Emilie F. Carlen
Emily Bronte
Emily Dickinson
Enid Bagnold
Enilor Macartney Lane
Erasmus W. Jones
Ernie Howard Pie
Ethel May Dell
Ethel Turner
Ethel Watts Mumford
Eugene Sue
Eugenie Foa
Eugene Wood
Eustace Hale Ball
Evelyn Everett-green
Everard Cotes
F. H. Cheley
F. J. Cross
F. Marion Crawford
Fannie E. Newberry
Federick Austin Ogg
Ferdinand Ossendowski
Fergus Hume
Florence A. Kilpatrick
Fremont B. Deering
Francis Bacon
Francis Darwin
Frances Hodgson Burnett
Frances Parkinson Keyes
Frank Gee Patchin
Frank Harris
Frank Jewett Mather
Frank L. Packard
Frank V. Webster
Frederic Stewart Isham
Frederick Trevor Hill
Frederick Winslow Taylor

Friedrich Kerst
Friedrich Nietzsche
Fyodor Dostoyevsky
G.A. Henty
G.K. Chesterton
Gabrielle E. Jackson
Garrett P. Serviss
Gaston Leroux
George A. Warren
George Ade
Geroge Bernard Shaw
George Cary Eggleston
George Durston
George Ebers
George Eliot
George Gissing
George MacDonald
George Meredith
George Orwell
George Sylvester Viereck
George Tucker
George W. Cable
George Wharton James
Gertrude Atherton
Gordon Casserly
Grace E. King
Grace Gallatin
Grace Greenwood
Grant Allen
Guillermo A. Sherwell
Gulielma Zollinger
Gustav Flaubert
H. A. Cody
H. B. Irving
H.C. Bailey
H. G. Wells
H. H. Munro
H. Irving Hancock
H. R. Naylor
H. Rider Haggard
H. W. C. Davis
Haldeman Julius
Hall Caine
Hamilton Wright Mabie
Hans Christian Andersen
Harold Avery
Harold McGrath
Harriet Beecher Stowe
Harry Castlemon
Harry Coghill
Harry Houidini

Hayden Carruth
Helent Hunt Jackson
Helen Nicolay
Hendrik Conscience
Hendy David Thoreau
Henri Barbusse
Henrik Ibsen
Henry Adams
Henry Ford
Henry Frost
Henry James
Henry Jones Ford
Henry Seton Merriman
Henry W Longfellow
Herbert A. Giles
Herbert Carter
Herbert N. Casson
Herman Hesse
Hildegard G. Frey
Homer
Honore De Balzac
Horace B. Day
Horace Walpole
Horatio Alger Jr.
Howard Pyle
Howard R. Garis
Hugh Lofting
Hugh Walpole
Humphry Ward
Ian Maclaren
Inez Haynes Gillmore
Irving Bacheller
Isabel Cecilia Williams
Isabel Hornibrook
Israel Abrahams
Ivan Turgenev
J.G.Austin
J. Henri Fabre
J. M. Barrie
J. M. Walsh
J. Macdonald Oxley
J. R. Miller
J. S. Fletcher
J. S. Knowles
J. Storer Clouston
J. W. Duffield
Jack London
Jacob Abbott
James Allen
James Andrews
James Baldwin

James Branch Cabell
James DeMille
James Joyce
James Lane Allen
James Lane Allen
James Oliver Curwood
James Oppenheim
James Otis
James R. Driscoll
Jane Abbott
Jane Austen
Jane L. Stewart
Janet Aldridge
Jens Peter Jacobsen
Jerome K. Jerome
Jessie Graham Flower
John Buchan
John Burroughs
John Cournos
John F. Kennedy
John Gay
John Glasworthy
John Habberton
John Joy Bell
John Kendrick Bangs
John Milton
John Philip Sousa
John Taintor Foote
Jonas Lauritz Idemil Lie
Jonathan Swift
Joseph A. Altsheler
Joseph Carey
Joseph Conrad
Joseph E. Badger Jr
Joseph Hergesheimer
Joseph Jacobs
Jules Vernes
Julian Hawthrone
Julie A Lippmann
Justin Huntly McCarthy
Kakuzo Okakura
Karle Wilson Baker
Kate Chopin
Kenneth Grahame
Kenneth McGaffey
Kate Langley Bosher
Kate Langley Bosher
Katherine Cecil Thurston
Katherine Stokes
L. A. Abbot
L. T. Meade

L. Frank Baum
Latta Griswold
Laura Dent Crane
Laura Lee Hope
Laurence Housman
Lawrence Beasley
Leo Tolstoy
Leonid Andreyev
Lewis Carroll
Lewis Sperry Chafer
Lilian Bell
Lloyd Osbourne
Louis Hughes
Louis Joseph Vance
Louis Tracy
Louisa May Alcott
Lucy Fitch Perkins
Lucy Maud Montgomery
Luther Benson
Lydia Miller Middleton
Lyndon Orr
M. Corvus
M. H. Adams
Margaret E. Sangster
Margret Howth
Margaret Vandercook
Margaret W. Hungerford
Margret Penrose
Maria Edgeworth
Maria Thompson Daviess
Mariano Azuela
Marion Polk Angellotti
Mark Overton
Mark Twain
Mary Austin
Mary Catherine Crowley
Mary Cole
Mary Hastings Bradley
Mary Roberts Rinehart
Mary Rowlandson
M. Wollstonecraft Shelley
Maud Lindsay
Max Beerbohm
Myra Kelly
Nathaniel Hawthrone
Nicolo Machiavelli
O. F. Walton
Oscar Wilde

Owen Johnson
P.G. Wodehouse
Paul and Mabel Thorne
Paul G. Tomlinson
Paul Severing
Percy Brebner
Percy Keese Fitzhugh
Peter B. Kyne
Plato
Quincy Allen
R. Derby Holmes
R. L. Stevenson
R. S. Ball
Rabindranath Tagore
Rahul Alvares
Ralph Bonehill
Ralph Henry Barbour
Ralph Victor
Ralph Waldo Emmerson
Rene Descartes
Ray Cummings
Rex Beach
Rex E. Beach
Richard Harding Davis
Richard Jefferies
Richard Le Gallienne
Robert Barr
Robert Frost
Robert Gordon Anderson
Robert L. Drake
Robert Lansing
Robert Lynd
Robert Michael Ballantyne
Robert W. Chambers
Rosa Nouchette Carey
Rudyard Kipling
Saint Augustine
Samuel B. Allison
Samuel Hopkins Adams
Sarah Bernhardt
Sarah C. Hallowell
Selma Lagerlof
Sherwood Anderson
Sigmund Freud
Standish O'Grady
Stanley Weyman
Stella Benson
Stella M. Francis

Stephen Crane
Stewart Edward White
Stijn Streuvels
Swami Abhedananda
Swami Parmananda
T. S. Ackland
T. S. Arthur
The Princess Der Ling
Thomas A. Janvier
Thomas A Kempis
Thomas Anderton
Thomas Bailey Aldrich
Thomas Bulfinch
Thomas De Quincey
Thomas Dixon
Thomas H. Huxley
Thomas Hardy
Thomas More
Thornton W. Burgess
U. S. Grant
Upton Sinclair
Valentine Williams
Various Authors
Vaughan Kester
Victor Appleton
Victor G. Durham
Victoria Cross
Virginia Woolf
Wadsworth Camp
Walter Camp
Walter Scott
Washington Irving
Wilbur Lawton
Wilkie Collins
Willa Cather
Willard F. Baker
William Dean Howells
William le Queux
W. Makepeace Thackeray
William W. Walter
William Shakespeare
Winston Churchill
Yei Theodora Ozaki
Yogi Ramacharaka
Young E. Allison
Zane Grey